DISNEP

BEAUTY
AND THE
BEAST

Beauty AND THE Beast

Adapted by Elizabeth Rudnick

Screenplay by STEPHEN CHBOSKY
and EVAN SPILIOTOPOULOS

DISNEP PRESS

LOS ANGELES · NEW YORK

Copyright © 2017 Disney Enterprises, Inc.

All rights reserved. Published by Disney Press, an imprint of
Disney Book Group. No part of this book may be reproduced or
transmitted in any form or by any means, electronic or mechanical,
including photocopying, recording, or by any information storage and
retrieval system, without written permission from the publisher.
For information address Disney Press, 1101 Flower Street,
Glendale, California 91201.

Printed in the United States of America
First Paperback Edition, January 2017
7 9 10 8
FAC-025438-17153

Library of Congress Control Number: 2016952935

ISBN 978-1-4847-8100-5

disneybooks.com

SUSTAINABLE
FORESTRY
INITIATIVE

Certified Chain of Custody
Promoting Sustainable Forestry

www.sfiprogram.org
SFI-01054

The SFI label applies to the text stock

AS ALL FAIRY TALES DO, THIS STORY begins with the simplest of words: once upon a time. . . . But that is where our story, a different type of fairy tale, takes a turn. For this is not just the tale of a beautiful maiden and a handsome prince—although, in truth, the lady is lovely and the prince can indeed be charming. This is a tale of a beauty much deeper than that. It is the story of two people drawn together under the most interesting of circumstances, two people who learn to truly see what matters only after they meet each other and their tale—one both as old as time and as fresh as a rose—begins.

So our story starts, once upon a time, in the hidden heart of France. . . .

PROLOGUE

THE PRINCE SCOWLED. HE FACED A pair of heavy gilded doors that were shut to him. From beyond, he could hear music and laughter. The party, *his party*, had already begun. Crystal clinked as guests toasted the night and wandered about the ornate ballroom, their eyes no doubt widening as they took in the hundreds of priceless objects that lined the walls. Beautiful vases, detailed portraits of faraway places, rich tapestries, and solid-gold serving plates were just a few of the many items. And they all paled in comparison to the beauty of the guests themselves. For the Prince did not invite just anyone to his parties. He invited only those he deemed beautiful enough to be in his presence. So they came from all over the world, each one as much on display as the inanimate objects in the room.

Standing in front of the closed doors, the Prince barely noticed the servants as they bustled about him, nervously putting the finishing touches on his costume. His majordomo hovered nearby, pocket watch in hand. The stuffy older man hated the Prince's utter lack of respect for time. In turn, the Prince took great pleasure in wasting the majordomo's. A maid stood next to the Prince, a feather brush in her hand. Gingerly, she painted a white line on the young man's face. The paint glided onto his smooth, flawless skin with ease. Finished, the maid pulled back her hand and cocked her head to the side as she took in her work.

The mask had taken hours to paint, and it showed. It was exquisite. The Prince's face had been transformed by the pale veil of paint. No detail had been spared, down to the faintest tracings of gold feathering and blue accents around his eyes and the dusting of rouge that sharpened his already striking cheekbones. Matching the latest fashion, two beauty marks had been perfectly placed—one beneath his right eye and one above his crimson lips. Underneath the masquerade makeup, the Prince's blue eyes shone coolly.

Stepping back, the maid waited as the head valet draped a long jeweled coat over the Prince's shoulders and then carefully inspected it to make sure not one jewel was out of place. Satisfied, he nodded at the maid, who then dusted the Prince's wig with powder. Then both bowed and waited with bated breath for the Prince to act.

Lifting one gloved hand, the Prince gave a single haughty wave. Instantly, a footman appeared. "More light," the Prince ordered.

"Yes, Your Highness," the footman said, turning and reaching for the candelabrum placed nearby. He lifted it so it illuminated the Prince's face.

The Prince held a small mirror. It was silver, with flourishes along the back and a delicate handle. In his large hands, the mirror looked tiny and incredibly fragile. Holding it up so he could see his face, the Prince preened. He turned left, then right, then left again before looking straight on at his reflection. He nodded once, and then, as though it were only a dishrag, the Prince dropped the mirror.

The maid, who had nearly fainted in relief at the Prince's nod of approval, gasped as the mirror began to fall. Not even bothering to turn at the noise, the Prince had the majordomo open the doors to the ballroom. As he entered, the footman lunged forward, catching the mirror just before it hit the floor. The servants let out a collective sigh as the doors swung shut behind the Prince. For the next few hours they would be able to relax, out of sight of their cruel, spoiled, and unkind master.

Unaware of his servants' thoughts, or perhaps aware but unconcerned, the Prince made his way across the ballroom. It was a sea of white—per his invitation. Many of the guests were hard to distinguish, save their masks. The result was enchanting. His mouth remained pulled down, however, and his solemn expression did not indicate any pleasure at seeing such beauty in his castle. He never allowed others to see if he felt joy or pain. It afforded him a sense of mystery, which he enjoyed immensely. As he walked, he heard the whispers of young women wondering excitedly if this would be the night he singled them out for a dance. A smug smile tugged at his lips, but he tamped it down and continued on his way.

Pushing through a circle of eligible maidens and their chaperones, the Prince arrived at his throne. It was raised above the ballroom floor, allowing him the best spot from which to view the party. Like everything else in the room, the throne was decadent in its design. A huge majestic coat of arms dominated the seat, making it clear, if it weren't already, whose throne it was. Standing beside it, the Prince turned and stared out at the ballroom. He watched a small animated man sit at the grand harpsichord across the room. The Prince locked eyes with the man, who smiled kindly in return, flashing teeth that had seen better days. The Prince grimaced but nodded. This was, after all, the premier

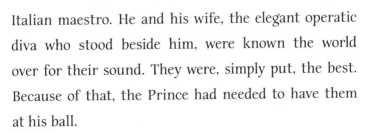

Italian maestro. He and his wife, the elegant operatic diva who stood beside him, were known the world over for their sound. They were, simply put, the best. Because of that, the Prince had needed to have them at his ball.

With the Prince's nod, the maestro began to play and the diva began to sing, her voice filling the ballroom. The Prince strode out onto the floor and started to dance. His moves were smooth and practiced, honed from years of training. Around him, ladies moved in reverse to the Prince, their dancing equally well practiced and smooth. Yet somehow they paled in comparison to him. His presence was bigger than the ballroom, his looks more beautiful, his coldness more chilling than the wind and rain that howled outside.

The diva's voice had just swelled to an almost painful note when, suddenly, above the music and over the wind, the Prince heard the unmistakable sound of someone knocking at the door that led out to the gardens. He lifted his hand, and the music came to an abrupt stop.

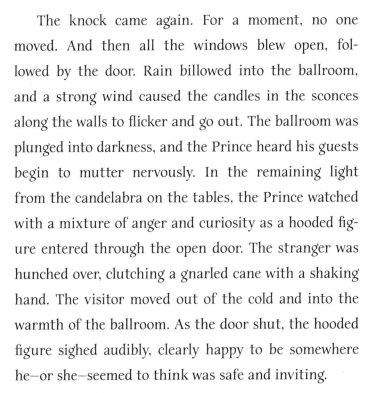

The knock came again. For a moment, no one moved. And then all the windows blew open, followed by the door. Rain billowed into the ballroom, and a strong wind caused the candles in the sconces along the walls to flicker and go out. The ballroom was plunged into darkness, and the Prince heard his guests begin to mutter nervously. In the remaining light from the candelabra on the tables, the Prince watched with a mixture of anger and curiosity as a hooded figure entered through the open door. The stranger was hunched over, clutching a gnarled cane with a shaking hand. The visitor moved out of the cold and into the warmth of the ballroom. As the door shut, the hooded figure sighed audibly, clearly happy to be somewhere he—or she—seemed to think was safe and inviting.

That couldn't have been more wrong.

His initial shock fading, the Prince felt rage well up inside him. Grabbing a candelabrum from a nearby table, he stormed through the crowd, pushing people out of his path. By the time he arrived at the door, his face was red, despite the layers of face paint. He noticed that the uninvited guest was an old beggar woman. Hunched as she was, the Prince towered over her.

"What is the meaning of this?" he demanded with a snarl.

The old woman looked up at him with hope in her eyes. Holding out a single red rose, she said in no more than a whisper, "I'm seeking shelter from the bitter storm outside." As if on cue, the wind rose to a fever pitch, howling like a mad beast.

The Prince remained unmoved.

He did not care if the woman was cold and wet. She was haggard, old, and a vagrant. And worse still, she was ruining his ball. Another wave of red-hot anger washed over him as he saw the ugliness amid all the beauty he had so carefully and painstakingly created. "Get out!" he sneered, waving her away with his hand. "Get out now. You do not belong here." He gestured around the room at the elegantly dressed guests.

"Please," the old woman begged. "I am only asking for shelter for one night. I will not even stay in the ballroom."

The Prince's frown deepened. "Don't you see, old woman? This is a place of beauty," he said, his voice cold. "You are too ugly for my castle. For my world. For me." The woman seemed to shrink as the Prince's words tore into her, but the Prince did not appear to have any remorse. Signaling to his majordomo and the head footman, he ordered the woman escorted out.

"You should not be deceived by appearances," the woman said as the two servants approached. "Beauty is found within. . . ."

The Prince threw back his head and laughed cruelly. "Say what you will, hag. But we all know what beautiful looks like—and it is not you. Now go!"

Turning, the Prince moved to leave. But a gasp from his guests gave him pause. As he looked over his shoulder, his eyes grew wide. Something was happening to the old woman. Her dirty cape and hood seemed to engulf her in a cocoon of sorts until she all but disappeared. Then a flash of light erupted, blinding him.

When his vision cleared, the old beggar was gone. In her place was the most beautiful woman the Prince had ever seen. She was floating above him, emitting a dazzling golden light not unlike the sun's. Instantly, the Prince knew exactly what she was, for he had read about such things. She was an enchantress—a woman of magic who had put him to a test.

And he had failed.

Falling to his knees, the Prince held up his hands. "Please," he said, now the one to beg. "I'm sorry, Enchantress. You are welcome in my castle for as long as you like."

The Enchantress shook her head. She had seen enough to know that it was a hollow apology. The Prince had no kindness or love in his heart. Magic coursed through her and then washed over the Prince.

The transformation began instantly. The Prince's body was racked with pain. His back arched and he groaned as his body began to grow. His jewelry popped off. His clothes ripped. The surrounding guests screamed at the sight of their host and fled. The Prince reached up, trying to grasp a nearby man's hand, but to his horror, he discovered his own hand resembled that of a monster. The man jumped away and made his escape, along with the others.

Amid it all, the Enchantress calmly watched her punishment take effect. Soon the ballroom was empty save for the staff, the entertainers, and a lone dog that belonged to the diva. As they looked on in shock, the Prince's transformation became complete. Where once there had towered a handsome man now cowered a hideous beast. But he was not the only one to have transformed. The rest of the castle and its inhabitants no longer looked the same. They, too, had changed. . . .

The days bled into years, and the Prince and his servants were forgotten by the world until, finally, the enchanted castle stood isolated and locked in perpetual winter. The Enchantress erased all memory of the castle and those who were in it, even from the minds of the people who loved them.

But there did remain one last bit of hope: the rose

she had offered the Prince was truly an enchanted rose. If the Prince could learn to love another and earn that person's love in return by the time the last petal fell, the spell would be broken. If not, he would be doomed to remain a beast forever.

CHAPTER I

BELLE OPENED THE FRONT DOOR OF her cottage. Taking in the picture-perfect pastoral scene in front of her, she sighed. Morning in the small village of Villeneuve began the same way each day. At least it had for as long as Belle had lived there.

The sun would rise slowly over the horizon, its rays turning the fields that surrounded the village more green or gold or white, depending on the season. Then the rays would move along until they touched the whitewashed sides of Belle's cottage, which stood right on the outskirts of the village, before finally illuminating the thatched roofs of the homes and shops that made up the village itself. By the time that happened, the villagers themselves would be stirring, preparing for the day. Inside their homes, men would sit down for their morning meals while the women readied the children or finished stirring the porridge. The village would be hushed, as though still shaking off sleep.

Then the clock on the church would strike eight.

And just like that, the village would come alive.

Belle had watched it happen hundreds of times. Yet this morning, like every morning, it still amazed her as she stared down at the little town, full of the same people going about their daily routines. Narrowing her warm brown eyes, she sighed at the mundanity of it all. She often wondered what it would be like to wake up differently.

Belle shook her head. It did her no good to wonder or wish. This was life as she'd always known it, the life she had shared with her papa ever since they had moved from Paris many years earlier. It was a waste of time to dwell on the past or the what-ifs. She had things to do, errands to run, and—she looked down at the book clutched in her hand—a new adventure to find. Straightening her shoulders, Belle pulled the door closed behind her and set off into town.

Within minutes, Belle was making her way down the cobblestoned main street. As she passed other villagers, she nodded distantly. While she had lived in the village most of her life, she still felt like a stranger there. It, like so many in the rural French countryside, was isolated and insular. Most of the people Belle passed on her way had been born there and most would spend the rest of their lives there. To them, the village was the world. And outsiders were viewed with caution.

Belle wasn't entirely sure that even if she had been born in the village she wouldn't still have been treated as an outsider. She really didn't have much in common with most of the others. And if she was being honest, she tended to enjoy reading more than idle small talk–traveling to distant lands and having wondrous adventures, even if only in the pages of her favorite books.

Weaving her way through the street, she listened

as the rest of the villagers greeted each other. She felt a pang of loneliness watching them talk to one another. They all seemed perfectly content with the monotony of their morning routines. No one seemed to share her desire for something new and exciting, for something *more*.

Belle reached the baker's stand, the sweet smell of freshly baked bread wafting through the air. As always, the harried baker was holding a tray of freshly made baguettes and muttering to himself. "Bonjour," Belle said. The man nodded absently.

"One baguette . . ." Belle peered at the row of jars filled with rich red jam. "And this, too, *s'il vous plaît*," she said, picking one up and sliding it into her apron pocket. After she'd paid and collected her goods, she moved on to complete her next errand.

She was just about to turn a corner when she paused. Jean, the old potter, was standing next to his mule looking confused. The cart attached to the mule was loaded with freshly made pottery. Looking up, Jean caught Belle watching him and smiled.

"Good morning, Belle," he said, his voice scratchy with age. He was peering into his cart, a puzzled expression on his face.

"Good morning, Monsieur Jean," Belle said in return. "Have you lost something again?"

The older man nodded. "I believe I have. Problem is, I can't remember what," he said sadly. Then he shrugged. "Well, I'm sure it will come to me." He turned and pulled on the mule's reins, trying to lead the stubborn animal away. The mule was having none of it. He tried to stick his nose in Belle's pocket, searching for the apple she had hidden there just in case she ran into Jean. Giving the creature a hard yank, Jean succeeded in drawing the mule's attention away from Belle. But he *also* succeeded in knocking the cart off balance.

Gasping, Belle reached out and grabbed one of the beautiful clay pots just before it fell. Then, satisfied nothing else would fall, she gave the mule the apple and turned to leave.

"Where are you off to?" Jean asked.

She looked back over her shoulder. "To return this

book to Pere Robert," she said, smiling and holding up the well-worn book. "It's about two lovers in fair Verona—"

"Are either of them potters?" Jean interrupted.

Belle shook her head. "No."

"Sounds boring," he said.

Belle sighed. She wasn't surprised by Jean's reaction. It was the same reaction she got anytime she mentioned books. Or art. Or travel. Or Paris. Anything other than talk of the village or the villagers was met with indifference—or, worse, disdain.

Just once, Belle thought as she patted Jean's mule on the nose and gave the potter a wave good-bye, *I'd like to meet someone who wanted to hear the story of Romeo and Juliet. Or any story, for that matter.* She started to walk more quickly, more eager than ever to get to Pere Robert's, get a new book, and return home. At least in her own cottage, she had no one to bother her or judge her. She could just get lost in her stories and imagine the world beyond the provincial town.

Absorbed in thoughts of what new bookish delights

might be awaiting her at Pere Robert's, Belle didn't even notice the attention she was getting. Nor did she pay any mind to the barely concealed comments her presence sparked. She had heard them all before. It was not the first time she had passed by the school and heard the young boys call her strange. The washer-women, their hands pruned and covered in suds, also loved to whisper among themselves whenever they saw Belle. "Funny girl," they would say. "Doesn't fit in" was another favorite. To the gossipy women, this was the worst offense of all. It never occurred to them that Belle *chose* not to be part of the crowd.

Finally, Belle arrived at her destination—the vestry of the church. Pushing open the doors, she breathed a sigh of relief as the quiet and serenity of the building enveloped her. The hubbub and noise of outside faded away, and for the first time that morning, Belle felt at peace. Hearing her enter, a kind man in a long black robe looked up from his book. The man was tall and slender, with warm eyes that crinkled as he smiled at Belle.

"Good morning, Belle," Pere Robert greeted her. "So where did you run off to this week?"

Belle smiled in return. The well-read priest was one of two people in the entire village Belle felt she could talk to. The other person was her father. "Two cities in Northern Italy," she answered, her tone growing animated. She held out the book, as if showing Pere Robert would somehow help bring the story fully to life. "You should have seen it. The castles. The art. There was even a masquerade ball."

Reaching out, Pere Robert took the book gingerly from Belle. He nodded as she continued to tell him the story of Romeo and Juliet as though he had never heard it before, even though they both knew he had read the story at least a dozen times himself. It was just part of their ritual. When she was done, Belle took a deep satisfied breath. "Have you got any new places to go?" she asked hopefully. She turned and her eyes lingered on the town's library.

Calling it a library was an exaggeration, to say the least. A few dozen books lined two small dusty bookshelves. Scanning the shelves now, Belle saw the same well-worn spines and faded titles. It was rare for anything to be added to the inventory.

"I'm afraid not," he replied. Despite the fact that she had anticipated this, Belle's eyes showed her disappointment. "But you may reread any of the old ones that you'd like," he added kindly.

Belle nodded and moved in front of the shelves. Her fingers brushed the familiar books, most of which she had read at least two times. Still, she knew better than to complain. Picking one up, she smiled back at the older man. "Thank you," she said softly. "Your library makes our small corner of the world almost feel big."

Book in hand, Belle left the vestry and made her way back out onto the village's main street. Opening to the first page, she planted her nose firmly in the book and blocked out everything else. She ducked under the cheese vendor carrying his tray of goods and swooped out of the way of the two florists, their arms loaded with huge bouquets, all the while never losing her spot on the page.

While she had been disappointed not to find any-thing new, this book *was* one of her favorites. It had everything a good story should have—far-off places, a charming prince, a strong heroine who discovered love . . . but not right away, of course.

CLANG! CLANG!

Startled by the loud noise, Belle finally tore herself from the book. Looking up, she saw that the noise was coming from Agathe. If the town thought Belle was odd, they considered the older woman an outcast. She had no home or family and spent her days begging for spare change and food. Looking past the dirt that covered her cheeks and the rags she wore, Belle had always had a soft spot for Agathe. She felt Agathe deserved as much care and respect as anyone else, and hated to see other villagers ignore Agathe, or—worse—mock her among themselves. Whenever she saw Agathe, Belle tried to give her a little something.

"Good morning, Agathe," she said now, smiling gen-tly. "I have no money. But here . . ." She reached into her bag, pulled out the baguette she had picked up especially for the older woman, and handed it over.

Agathe smiled gratefully. Then her smile turned playful. "No jam?" Anticipating the response, Belle already had her hand in her pocket and produced the jar of jam. "Bless you," Agathe said. Lowering her head, she ripped a chunk off the baguette, Belle's presence instantly forgotten.

Belle smiled. She felt, in some strange way, a kinship with the woman. Agathe simply wanted to have food and be left alone. Belle was the same way with her books. As lonely as she could be at times, she couldn't stand unwanted attention—hated it, in fact.

CHAPTER II

GASTON LOVED ATTENTION. HE LIVED for it, in fact. Ever since he had been a small boy, he had sought out ways to make himself the center of attention. He walked before anyone else his age. He talked first, and as he got older, he grew taller and more handsome than anyone else. With his dark hair, piercing eyes, and broad shoulders, he was indeed good-looking. The girls loved him; the boys worshiped him. And Gaston? He soaked up the attention and reveled in it.

But there was a limit to just how much attention Gaston could get growing up in a small village. And it had irked him. Then, to his great delight, France had gotten involved in the war. Gaston had seen the war not as an opportunity to defend his country but as a chance to wear a dashing uniform and woo the ladies, which he had done, with gusto, when he became a certified war hero—twelve years ago.

Gaston still wore his uniform.

And he *still* believed himself the most handsome and manliest man in the entire village.

Now he sat astride his large black stallion, staring down at his village from the promontory that overlooked it. His chest bulged beneath a dazzling gold breastplate. The muscles on his arms rippled as he pulled back on the horse's reins, making the animal dance nervously. Strapped to his saddle were his trusty musket and the spoils of his hunt. As usual, he'd had a successful afternoon in the woods.

"You didn't miss a shot, Gaston," said the man beside him.

If Gaston was a lion of a man, which many a person had called him over the years, the man beside him was a house cat. LeFou was everything Gaston was not. Where Gaston was tall and muscled, LeFou was short and soft. Where Gaston was all smooth, practiced moves and well-rehearsed lines, LeFou was stumbling

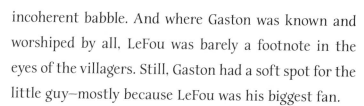

incoherent babble. And where Gaston was known and worshiped by all, LeFou was barely a footnote in the eyes of the villagers. Still, Gaston had a soft spot for the little guy—mostly because LeFou was his biggest fan.

"You're the greatest hunter in the village," LeFou went on. Gaston shot him a look and he quickly corrected himself. "I mean . . . the *world*."

Gaston puffed out his already puffed-out chest even more and raised his chin in the air, as though posing for an unseen artist. "Thank you, LeFou," he said. He looked down at what LeFou had "caught"—a handful of vegetables—and raised an eyebrow. "You didn't do too badly yourself," he added insincerely.

"One of these days I'm going to learn to shoot like you," LeFou said, oblivious to Gaston's mockery. "And talk like you. And be tall and handsome like you."

"Come now, old friend," Gaston said, pretending not to love every compliment. "Reflected glory is just as good as the real thing."

LeFou cocked his head, confused. He opened his mouth to speak but stopped when he saw Gaston sit up straighter in his saddle. The dark-haired man's eyes narrowed, as if he were a wolf spotting his prey. Following Gaston's gaze, LeFou saw what had caught his friend's attention. Below, Belle was making her way through the village square. Her bright blue dress was flattering against her rich auburn hair. Even from such a distance, LeFou could see that her cheeks were flushed becomingly.

"Look at her, LeFou," Gaston went on. "My future wife. Belle is the most beautiful girl in the village. That makes *her* the best."

"But she's so well read, and you're so . . ." LeFou caught himself. He had almost just done the one thing he prided himself on *never* doing—offending Gaston. Quickly, before Gaston could wonder about the hesitation, he finished his sentence. "Athletically inclined."

Gaston nodded. "I know," he agreed. "Belle can be as argumentative as she is beautiful."

"Exactly!" LeFou said, happy to see his friend talking with some sense. "Who needs her? You've got us!

Le Duo!" He threw out the nickname almost hopefully. When they had first returned home from the war—because of course LeFou had gone with his pal to fight—the little man had tried in vain to get the village to call the pair *Le Duo*. But it had never stuck. It was usually Gaston and "the other one." Or more often than not, just Gaston.

Absorbed in himself, Gaston barely registered the neediness in his friend's voice. "Ever since the war, I've been missing something," he said, still looking at Belle. "And she's the only girl I've met who gives that sense of . . ." Gaston stumbled, trying to find the right words.

"Je ne sais quoi?" LeFou finished for him.

Gaston turned and looked at him, confusion on his face. "I don't know what that means," he said. "I just know that from the moment I saw her, I knew I would marry Belle. And I don't want to stand here any longer, wasting time." Kicking his horse into a gallop, he headed toward the village, the picture of a hero returning from war. Behind him, LeFou spurred his pony's sides. The furry animal pinned back its ears and broke right into . . . a slow trot.

Belle heard the sound of hoofbeats moments before the horses burst through the village gates. In truth, one burst through; the other sort of meandered. Instantly, Belle recognized the large black stallion and the man astride its back. It was Gaston. Behind him, his ever-present sidekick, LeFou, was struggling to keep up on his shaggy pony. She stifled a groan and quickly ducked behind the cheese seller, hoping Gaston would not notice her.

She'd had one too many run-ins with the war hero. Every time, it went the same way. Gaston would preen like a peacock while he boasted of his latest hunt or told her a tale from his glory days in the war. Belle would try not to roll her eyes. The villagers—especially the female ones—would swoon and whisper how lucky Belle was, and ultimately, Belle would walk away feeling the need to bathe. She knew that Gaston was considered by many—well, *all* if she was being honest—to be quite the catch. But she just couldn't stand the man. There was something *beastly* about him.

Like now, she thought as she peeked out from behind the *fromagerie.* Gaston was clutching flowers in his hand and scanning the crowd like a wild animal. Belle groaned as his eyes locked on hers and he began to push through the villagers to get to her. She turned and hurried off in the opposite direction, hoping the other villagers would distract him.

Unbeknownst to Belle, just as Gaston was about to reach her, Agathe stepped in front of him, her cup raised. Gaston looked down at the homeless woman and his lips curled. Then he saw the shiny metal cup. "Thank you, hag," he said, grabbing it out of her hands and turning it upside down. Coins spilled to the ground as Gaston checked out his reflection in the bottom of the mug. Satisfied with what he saw, he shoved the cup back at Agathe and moved past her.

"Good morning, Belle," he said, running to come to a stop in front of her. She took a step backward. "Wonderful book you have there."

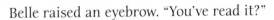

Belle raised an eyebrow. "You've read it?"

"I did a lot of things in the army," he answered vaguely.

Belle swallowed a laugh. It had taken him less than a minute to bring up the army. *Must be a record*, she thought.

With a flourish, Gaston presented the flowers. "For your dinner table," he explained. "Shall I join you tonight?"

"Sorry," Belle said hastily, shaking her head. She inched around him, looking for the quickest escape route. "Not tonight."

"Busy?" Gaston asked.

"No," Belle said, and then before Gaston could reply or process her refusal, she was ducking back out into the street. Behind her, she heard Gaston twisting her words for the audience of villagers who had stopped to watch the pair. It was clear that the hunter had interpreted her no as part of a game of hard to get.

She didn't care what Gaston said or how he made

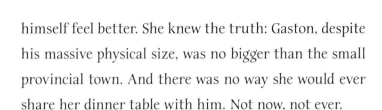

himself feel better. She knew the truth: Gaston, despite his massive physical size, was no bigger than the small provincial town. And there was no way she would ever share her dinner table with him. Not now, not ever.

Quickening her pace, Belle made her way out of the village center. Moments later she arrived back at her cottage. It was a cozy little house, with a small staircase leading up to the front door and large picture windows. There was also a nice garden out front and a detached basement workshop for her father.

The soft tinkling melody of a music box drifted up from the closed hatch doors. Her father was already working, despite the early hour.

Careful not to disturb him, Belle opened the hatch and tiptoed down the stairs. Sunlight streamed through a small window, illuminating Maurice as he sat hunched over his workbench. Bits and pieces of his projects were scattered about. Small knobs, tiny screws, half-painted boxes, and delicate figurines sat on various shelves and tables. Some were newer, their surfaces

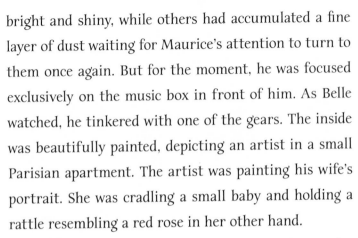

bright and shiny, while others had accumulated a fine layer of dust waiting for Maurice's attention to turn to them once again. But for the moment, he was focused exclusively on the music box in front of him. As Belle watched, he tinkered with one of the gears. The inside was beautifully painted, depicting an artist in a small Parisian apartment. The artist was painting his wife's portrait. She was cradling a small baby and holding a rattle resembling a red rose in her other hand.

Belle took a step farther into the room. Maurice looked up distractedly at the sound. Seeing his daughter, he smiled. His eyes, the same warm color as Belle's, were bright and focused. When he straightened his shoulders, he grew taller and leaner, still handsome in his older age. "Oh, good, Belle, you're back," he said, turning again to the music box. "Where were you?"

"Well, first I went to Saint Petersburg to see the tsar, then I went fishing in the bottom of the well," she began, smiling as he nodded absently. When he was working, he didn't see or hear anything else. Belle understood.

She was the same way when she was entranced by a book.

"Hmmm, yes," Maurice said. "Can you please hand me the—"

Before he could finish, Belle was handing him the screwdriver.

"And the—"

This time she held out a small hammer.

"No, I don't need . . ." His voice trailed off as a spring popped off. "Well, yes, I guess I do."

As he went back to tinkering, Belle walked over to a shelf full of completed music boxes. Her long thin fingers trailed over them as she moved down the row. Each one was a piece of art, depicting famous landmarks from around the world. She knew her father made them for her, as a way to give her a glimpse beyond the village. Maurice never said as much, but Belle knew he was aware of her longing to explore, to get out of the small world where he felt she was safe. She thought of the small village and the gossiping people who lived there.

Softly, so as not to startle him, Belle asked, "Papa, do you think I'm odd?"

Hearing her tone, Maurice looked up from his work. He frowned. "Do I think you're odd?" he repeated. "Where did you get an idea like that?"

Belle shrugged. "Oh, I don't know. . . . People talk."

"There are worse things than being talked about," Maurice said, his tone growing sad. "This village may be small-minded, Belle, but it's also safe."

Belle opened her mouth to protest. That was the line her father used all the time. She knew it came from a good place, but she just didn't understand why he wanted to *stay* in their small town.

Seeing his typical explanation wasn't going to work on Belle today, Maurice quickly changed course. "Back in Paris," he said, "I knew a girl who was so different, so daring, so ahead of her time that people mocked her until the day they found themselves imitating her. Do you know what she used to say?"

Belle shook her head.

"She used to say, 'The people who talk behind your back are destined to stay there.'" Maurice paused for a moment, letting the words sink in. Then he added. *"Behind your back. Never to catch up."*

Slowly, Belle nodded. She enjoyed Maurice's little stories that served as life lessons. She had, in fact, thought she'd already heard them all. But this was a new one. Her father was trying to tell her it was all right to stand out, be apart from the crowd. She nodded once more. "I understand," she said softly.

"That woman was your mother," Maurice added, smiling and reaching out to take his daughter's hand. He gave it a squeeze.

Belle smiled back, warmth and sadness filling her heart. She didn't remember her mother. All she had were the stories her father told her. But remembering was hard on Maurice, so he gave her only snippets—like this one—from time to time. "Tell me more about her," Belle prompted as Maurice tried to return to his work. "Please. One more thing."

The older man's hand hovered over the music box. Slowly, his fingers closed and he looked back at his daughter. "Your mother was . . . fearless," he said. "To know anything more, you just have to look in the mirror." He picked up a pair of tweezers and placed the last gear in the music box. With a click, it snapped into place.

"It's beautiful," Belle said as music tinkled forth. As she looked up, her eyes landed on the portrait hanging above her father's workshop. It showed the same image that was depicted on the inside of the newest music box. Her mother was the woman holding the infant and the rose rattle. And Belle was the baby. It was the only image of her mother Belle knew. "I think she would have loved it," Belle added softly.

But her father didn't hear her. He was once again lost in the world of his music boxes. Belle knew that talking more about her mother would only sadden him. She turned and headed back upstairs. She loved her father so much, and she didn't want to cause him any more pain or heartache than he'd already experienced in his life. But sometimes she wondered if there was a chance anything would ever happen to set her life on a different path than the one she and her father were so firmly planted on now.

CHAPTER III

BELLE WAVED TO HER FATHER AS HE drove his cart away from their cottage. Philippe, their gentle giant of a draft horse, tossed his head in the air and whickered happily, ready for the adventure.

As he did every year, Maurice was heading to the large market a few towns over to sell his music boxes. The cart was loaded with every piece he had worked on for the past year, carefully packed and stored to protect them during the long journey. And as he did every year, Maurice was leaving Belle behind. It was for her own safety, he always told her. Or because he couldn't leave the cottage unattended, he would sometimes add. Either way, every time it was the same. He packed up the cart, Belle made sure Philippe was ready for the journey, and then they went through their ritual of saying good-bye. Belle would tuck Maurice's cravat into his shirt, and Maurice would ask Belle: "What would you like from the market?"

"A rose like the one in the painting," was always Belle's reply.

Then, after a quick hug and a pat for Philippe, Maurice would head out.

This year had been no different. When her father and Philippe were finally out of view, Belle sighed. *Well*, she thought as she walked back into the cottage, *now what?* She knew she could read or clean or work in the garden. But for some reason none of those things appealed to her at the moment. She needed to do something more. Something that would get her out of her own head—which was beginning to fill with worry about her father's trip, as it did every year. Catching sight of the large pile of laundry, she raised an eyebrow. Normally, she hated doing the laundry. The washerwomen were always by the fountain, gossiping and jabbering away. When she arrived, they would inevitably get louder, their laughter colder—lasting the excruciating length of time it took to get the clothes clean. If only it didn't take so long . . .

She looked around the room, noticing one of Philippe's leather harnesses and the basket of apples. Suddenly, she had a thought. Smiling, she ran into the barn, grabbed what she needed, and headed into the village. To her delight, when she arrived, the only person at the fountain was a young girl with sad eyes. Belle had seen the girl around the village before. She was always by herself, and judging by the way she hunched her shoulders and avoided eye contact, Belle was pretty sure she didn't have a lot of friends. As Belle watched, the girl plunged a shirt into the fountain and then pulled it out and began scrubbing at it.

Taking her pile to the fountain's edge, Belle began to pull her other supplies from her apron pockets. She walked over to Jean the potter's mule, which was standing by the door to the tavern with its head down, lips twitching, and one hind foot cocked. After attaching one end of Philippe's harness to the mule's halter, Belle secured the other end to a small wooden barrel. Then she dumped all the clothes and a few soap chips into the barrel before lifting it and dropping it right into the fountain. The barrel bobbed on its side, filling slowly with water. Belle walked in front of the mule. Holding up one of the apples enticingly, she walked backward. The mule followed. She set it on a path walking around the fountain.

"What are you doing?"

Belle saw that the girl was watching her, a perplexed look on her face.

"The laundry," Belle answered matter-of-factly. She pointed to the barrel. The mule was dragging it through the water, churning up the liquid and covering the clothes in a nice layer of suds. Satisfied with her work, Belle took her book out of one of her apron pockets and sat down to read. Glancing at the girl, who was eyeing the book with something close to hunger, Belle smiled. "Well, what are you waiting for?"

Belle wasn't sure how long she had been sitting by the fountain. Jean's mule was still doing laps, the water was less sudsy, and the clothes were much cleaner. But Belle barely registered any of that. She was too focused on the girl sitting beside her. She had spent the morning and some of the afternoon trying to teach her to read. She knew that the village elders frowned upon girls reading—hence the local school was open only to boys— but Belle had never agreed with that narrow-minded way of thinking. So when the girl had sat down on the fountain wall and asked in a voice barely above a whisper if Belle would tell her a story, Belle had been excited to be able to share the thrill of reading with her. The idea of living in this village and not being able to escape through books was alarming. And the girl lived that life every day. Belle was determined to change that.

They had gotten pretty far. The girl was much further along than Belle would have thought possible. She just needed practice.

"T . . . th . . . the blue bi-ir-ird flies . . ." the girl stammered.

"Over the dark wood," Belle prompted. She opened her mouth to read the next line but was interrupted by a shout from nearby. Looking up, Belle saw the thin cruel face of the headmaster in the school's doorway. She sighed. Their moment of peace and quiet seemed to be over.

"What on earth are you doing?" he shouted, storming over to her. A line of boys followed him, their matching uniforms making them look like a small army. "Girls don't read."

His shouts quickly garnered the attention of more villagers. Jean the potter appeared, followed by the fishmonger and even Pere Robert and Agathe. They waited to see what Belle would say or do.

Raising one perfectly arched eyebrow, Belle met the headmaster's angry gaze. For a moment, they remained that way, eyes locked. Then Belle turned back to the girl and smiled. "Try again," she said.

As if she had ignited a powder keg of explosives, the villagers who had gathered went off. Some, like the fishmonger and the headmaster, expressed outrage at Belle's audacious behavior. Others, like Pere Robert, cheered her on. Amid it all, Belle sat unbothered. *Let the headmaster scream and shout and throw a fit*, she thought.

He should *be concerned with his students' education.*

Suddenly, over the increasingly loud shouts of the villagers, a shot rang out.

Startled, Belle looked up. Then she rolled her eyes.

Gaston stood, or rather posed, with one hand on his hip and the other holding his hunting rifle to the sky. Smoke still wafted from the tip of the recently fired weapon. LeFou, ever the aide, was pushing his way through the villagers. "Make a lane, people," he shouted. "Come on, don't make me say it twice."

Walking behind him, Gaston lowered the rifle and handed it to LeFou. Then he looked over the crowd. "This is not how good people behave," he said, shaking his head. "Everyone . . . go home. *Now!*" If the gun hadn't been enough to get their attention, the man's deep bellow did the trick. The villagers, mumbling to each other, began to disperse. Within moments, the area around the fountain was almost empty. The only ones left were Belle, Gaston, and LeFou. Even the young girl had taken off, frightened by the war hero's shout.

Belle didn't know whether to laugh or cry. Gaston

surely thought he had just come to her rescue, but all he had done was given the other villagers what they'd wanted and ended her reading lesson. Not to mention frustrate her.

Belle got to her feet and walked away from the fountain. Gaston fell in step beside her. For a few glorious moments, the large man was silent as they walked toward Belle's cottage, and Belle wondered if perhaps she had been wrong. Maybe Gaston wouldn't make this all about him. And then he spoke.

"I was pretty great back there, wasn't I?" he said. "Like being back in command during the war . . ."

"That was twelve years ago, Gaston," Belle pointed out.

"Sad, I know," Gaston said, clearly missing Belle's tone. He slowed his steps, and his expression grew serious. "Belle, I'm sure you think I have it all. But there *is* something I'm missing."

Hoping to get away, Belle quickened her own pace. "I can't imagine . . ."

"A wife," Gaston went on, his tone earnest but the

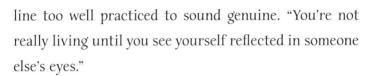

line too well practiced to sound genuine. "You're not really living until you see yourself reflected in someone else's eyes."

Oh, no, Belle thought. This was just what she had feared might happen. And she needed to nip any further talk of wives right in the bud. "And you can see yourself in mine?" she asked, trying to make her tone as disinterested and removed as possible.

Gaston nodded. "We're both fighters," he said, clearly referring to the incident at the fountain.

"All I wanted was to teach a child to read," Belle protested. *Not be a fighter,* she added silently.

"The only children you should concern yourself with are . . . your own."

Gaston's words hit Belle like a runaway cart. *As if he knows me, or what I want, at all,* she thought. *How dare he make assumptions?* She clenched her fists at her sides and tried to keep her voice steady as she said, "I'm not ready to have children."

"Maybe you haven't met the right man," Gaston responded.

"It's a small village," Belle shot back. "I've met them all."

"Maybe you should take a second look. . . ."

Belle shook her head. "I have."

"Maybe you should take a third look," Gaston went on, not picking up on the hint. "Some of us have changed."

Enough! Belle wanted to shout. Gaston could change into Mark Antony and she into Cleopatra and she *still* wouldn't want to be with him. Ever. Never, ever, *ever*. "Look," she finally said. "We could never make each other happy. No one can change *that* much." Picking up her pace still more, she tried to get away from Gaston. This conversation had gone on long enough. Up ahead, she could see the front door of her cottage, like a beacon of safety.

But Gaston wasn't having it. His long legs quickly closed the gap between them, his boots crushing the vegetables in the little garden. "Belle, do you know what happens to spinsters in our village after their fathers die?" he asked, the earlier softness of his voice

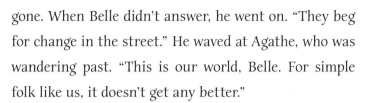

gone. When Belle didn't answer, he went on. "They beg for change in the street." He waved at Agathe, who was wandering past. "This is our world, Belle. For simple folk like us, it doesn't get any better."

"I may be a farm girl," Belle said, climbing the steps with Gaston close on her heels. She came to a stop and turned to look straight at him. "But I'm *not* simple. I'm sorry, but I will never marry you, Gaston."

Without another word, she pushed her way inside and firmly shut the door, preventing the hunter from following. She knew he couldn't have liked having a door slammed in his face, but he'd left her with no choice. Hopefully this would be the end of Gaston's unwanted advances.

Someday, she thought as she slumped against the door, *someday I'll find someone who will understand me, someone who will let me be me. Someday I'll show them all. I want so much more than the people in this town could ever understand.*

CHAPTER IV

IGHTNING FLASHED, ILLUMINATING the woods with a menacing white light. A moment later, the wind picked up. Leaves whipped across the ground at Philippe's feet as he trotted nervously forward. The horse's eyes bulged as a moment later a loud crack of thunder roared in the sky above. Jigging his head, he rattled his bit.

In his spot on the carriage's front seat, Maurice knew what the big animal was trying to say: *Let's turn around now, before it's too late.* But he also knew it already *was* too late. They had somehow gotten stuck in the middle of what locals called the dark forest. Rumors swirled around that thick patch of woods. Some said witches lived there. Others claimed it was full of packs of wolves smarter than most men. There were even those who said the trees had been known to speak. It was the type of place where one saw dark and hostile eyes wherever one looked.

It was *not* the type of place to get lost in at night—especially in the middle of a storm.

"Perhaps we should have turned *right* at those crossroads, old friend," Maurice said, his hands shaking on the reins as more lightning streaked the sky. "Or perhaps I should stop pretending my horse understands me."

Just then, another bolt of lightning flashed down. Only this time, it nearly hit Maurice and Philippe. It missed them, barely, but a gnarled and withered tree did not fare so well. The lightning tore it in two. As it split, one half fell onto the road right in front of Philippe. The other half fell sideways. When Maurice looked closer, he saw that the second half of the tree had fallen right next to a previously hidden narrow path.

Glancing back and forth, Maurice pondered what to do. A rational, reasonable part of him knew that he should find a way to keep going on the road. But a smaller part of him realized that was never going to happen. At least not that night. He couldn't get the cart, himself, and Philippe around the fallen tree. With a sigh, he tugged on the reins, steering his horse toward the path.

"It will be all right, Philippe," he said as the horse whinnied nervously. *I hope*, he added silently.

As they moved farther and farther down the path, Maurice became less and less confident that things would turn out well. The weather, which had already been stormy, grew worse—and stranger. Even though it was summer, a light whirling snow began to fall, dusting his jacket and turning Philippe's coat from dappled gray to white. It also grew eerily quiet. The rumbling of thunder vanished, and soon the only sound echoing through the seemingly empty woods was the clip-clop of Philippe's hooves.

And then there was a piercing howl.

An instant later a huge white wolf burst out of the bushes, barely missing the cart. Looking over, Maurice saw an entire pack of the beasts running parallel to them. "Go, Philippe!" he cried, slapping the reins against the horse's neck, as if the creature needed any encouragement. "Hurry!"

The horse wasted no time. He broke into a gallop. But the sudden movement combined terribly with the cart's age and general disrepair. Just as the horse started to pull away from the wolves, the cart began to buckle and the harness loosened. Within seconds, the cart tipped.

Maurice cried out as the cart fell to the ground and he was thrown into the air. He heard the sound of his beloved music boxes breaking as they fell and the slavering howls of the wolves, and he knew it was only a matter of time before he, too, fell and was destroyed. But just then, his plummeting body came to a jerking stop. Looking up, he saw that his descent had been stopped by a low-hanging limb. He dangled from it helplessly.

Shaking off the last bits of his leather harness, Philippe kicked out a hind leg, toppling one of the wolves. Seeing his owner hanging from the tree, he raced underneath it. Maurice didn't waste a minute. Reaching over his shoulder, he freed himself from the limb and fell onto the horse's back. Then, with a loud *h'yah*, he kicked the large animal forward.

As they raced through the woods, Maurice clung to Philippe's mane. The wolves followed, their eyes mad with hunger, their jaws open to reveal sharp teeth.

Just then, Maurice thought he saw something glimmer from the corner of his eye. Could there be some sort of structure . . . a safe haven in this godforsaken place? A moment later, he knew he hadn't imagined it. A huge ornate gate, frozen over with ice, had suddenly appeared in front of them. As they raced up to it, the gate swung open slightly. Philippe plunged through. The tip of his tail had only just made it inside the gate when it closed. Behind them, the wolves' howls turned to yelps of fear and then faded altogether as the creatures ran away.

If Maurice had not just barely escaped a pack of wolves with his life, he might have taken pause at their sudden disappearance—or the odd gate that opened and closed by itself. He might even have wondered *how* a castle as large and ornate as the one that rose in front of him could seem to appear out of nowhere. But as it was, he didn't stop to think about it. Instead, he kicked Philippe forward, toward the large castle and whoever lived inside.

Maurice had seen great buildings before. After all, he had lived the majority of his life in Paris, where beautiful buildings dominated the skyline. He had seen the artistry that went into creating such architectural wonders and, as an artist himself, was in awe of those who crafted their visions into reality. But nothing he had ever seen in Paris could have prepared him for the castle he saw now.

It seemed to defy gravity, with large turrets that reached high into the stormy sky. Its sides were made of gray stone cut so that it seemed the castle had grown out of the ground. The path Philippe now trotted on was actually a long bridge that spanned a frozen moat and ended in front of the castle's massive entryway. To the right of the huge front doors was a large colonnade. To Maurice's surprise, growing behind the colonnade, despite the strange cold weather, were beautiful rose-bushes. White roses blossomed on all of them, so pure that they even stood out against the snow.

A small shiver of fear flashed over Maurice. Roses growing in the snow? It was most unnatural. But as quickly as the feeling came, it went when Maurice noticed the castle's large stable. The door to the out-building was open and a lamp had been lit inside.

Maurice steered Philippe over, then quickly dismounted and led him inside the stable. He paused on the threshold and looked around. It seemed like an ordinary enough stable. "Water, fresh hay," Maurice observed, giving the large animal a pat. "Looks like you're set, old friend. Rest here"–he looked back outside to the castle beyond–"while I pay my respects to our host."

Turning, he headed across the courtyard and cautiously walked up the steps to what he assumed was the castle's front door. The tingle of fear returned as he gazed up at a row of torches held by hands sculpted from iron. The hands were so lifelike Maurice couldn't help reaching out and tapping one, just to be sure. The hand remained still. But the door did not. It swung open in front of him.

"Hello?" Maurice called, peering in. "Anyone home?"

His voice echoed through the large empty hall. Maurice could just make out the faint sound of a harpsichord coming from somewhere deep within the castle. Someone, it seemed, *was* home.

Letting out a nervous breath, Maurice walked inside. "Forgive me," he said as he went. "I don't mean to intrude. I need shelter from the storm. Hello?" Tall windows let in the faint light from outside, barely illuminating the castle's interior. Noticing a coatrack, Maurice took off his hat and coat and hung them to dry. With the cold layers gone, Maurice felt a bit better. He continued inside. Focused on what was in front of him, he didn't notice that as soon as his back was turned, the coatrack came to life, shaking the snow off Maurice's coat and hat like a dog shaking off the rain.

Maurice also failed to notice a large candelabrum

and ornate mantel clock sitting on a nearby table. As he passed them, the candelabrum slowly turned, watching the man.

"What are you doing?" the clock whispered as the candelabrum craned its neck. "Stop that!"

Instantly, the candelabrum stopped. But it was not because the mantel clock had told it to. It stopped because Maurice had heard the clock's barely hushed whisper and spun around.

For a tense moment, Maurice eyed the candelabrum and the clock. He approached the table on which they were placed and picked up the candelabrum. He held it up to the dim light and inspected it. He turned it upside down, then right side up. He shifted it to the left and then the right. Finally, he flicked it with his finger. *Ping, ping, ping.* Seemingly satisfied by the candelabrum's "candelabrum-ness," he put it back down on the table and moved on.

Behind him, the candelabrum rubbed its head, ignoring the "I told you so" look the clock was shooting at it.

Maurice continued his exploration of the castle. A grand staircase rose from the middle of the massive foyer. Almost tiptoeing—the huge empty space made Maurice feel even more like an intruder than he already had—he made his way behind the staircase. His heart beat faster when he noticed an entire wall covered in weapons of all sorts, shapes, and sizes. Whoever lived there, or had lived there, knew his armory.

Suddenly, Maurice again heard the faint sound of music being played. He followed the soft, slow melody, passing several closed doors before coming to a pair of large gilded doors that hung open. Inside, through the thick shadows, Maurice saw a ballroom of massive proportions. The music seemed to be coming from a dusty harpsichord in the corner. But as soon as Maurice took a step forward, the sound abruptly stopped.

"Hello?" Maurice called, peering into now silent room. Remnants of decorations, long since decayed, were strewn about, and when he squinted hard enough, Maurice could make out a hastily repaired window. But there was no sign of anyone, no musician seated on the harpsichord's bench. Maurice shook his head, wondering if he'd imagined the music.

Shivering, Maurice turned his back on the ballroom. In addition to the phantom music, there was something infinitely sad about the space. It was a room meant for joy and was now a room of disrepair and sadness. As he made his way back into the foyer, he couldn't help wondering what had happened there to give the ballroom such a feeling. Perhaps he had been hearing remnants of the past. Maurice had only just shrugged off the melancholy that had descended on him when, out of the corner of his eye, he saw someone lunging toward him.

Maurice recoiled in fear, his breath catching in his throat. But a moment later, he let out that breath as he realized what he had seen was simply his own reflection. A broken mirror hung on the wall. In the center was a large hole, with long shards of glass radiating from it, as though the mirror had been struck by a fist. The hole had distorted Maurice's reflection. He stared at his face, the lines around his eyes made deeper, his nose moved from the center to the left. He raised a hand to his cheek, as if to check that it was in fact just the reflection, not an actual change in his appearance.

As he did so, Maurice heard the sound of a fire crackling from somewhere close by. Turning, he saw an open door, through which he could make out a welcoming light. He looked down at his hands. They were shaking with a chill that had returned upon his seeing the eerie mirror. Without a second thought, he made his way into the room. To his delight, the fire he had heard was huge. It roared inside a large ornate hearth.

"Aaah, that's better," Maurice said, moving in front of the flames and holding out his hands. "So much better . . ." When his front felt sufficiently warmed, he turned to heat his backside. His eyes widened. Off the room he was in was yet another room. And in *that* room was a long dining table covered in an elaborate—and decidedly delicious-smelling—feast. Maurice's stomach growled.

Looking to see if he had missed other guests and

finding none, Maurice left the warmth of the fire to stand in front of the table. His stomach growled again. He knew he probably shouldn't . . . but he couldn't stop himself. He tore a hunk of bread off a massive loaf and then cut a healthy chunk of cheese from an even healthier wheel. "Do you mind . . . I'm just going to help myself . . . ?" he called out to the unseen host of the dinner. His mouth was full, so the words came out a bit garbled. He looked down at the table, hoping to see something refreshing. His eyes landed on a delicate china teacup full of an amber liquid. He was lifting it to his mouth when . . .

"Mom said I wasn't supposed to move because it might be scary."

Maurice nearly dropped the cup. Had it just spoken to him?

"Sorry."

Maurice yelped. Apparently, the cup—the cup made of china . . . the cup full of tea . . . the cup that was supposed to be just a cup—*had* spoken to him. Twice.

In the next instant, Maurice did what any man in

his position would do when confronted with a talking teacup. He turned and ran toward the front door. Grabbing his hat and coat from the coatrack, he bowed, his manners taking over despite the fear coursing through him. "Thank you," he called out to the shadows. "Really, I cannot thank you enough for your hospitality . . . and kindness." Then, his duty as a gentleman done, he slipped out the door and raced into the darkness toward the stable.

Inside one of the stalls, Philippe stood chewing a mouthful of hay. Seeing his owner tearing inside, he shifted nervously on his big feet. Throwing the reins over Philippe's head, Maurice led him out of the stall, eager to get away from the strange castle once and for all. But as he made his way back toward the gate, Maurice's attention was caught once more by the rose-filled colonnade. He *had* promised Belle a rose. For some reason, he felt it was especially important to return with the gift this time.

Stopping, Maurice gave Philippe a reassuring pat on

the neck and slipped inside the garden. Neither man nor horse noticed the dark shape that darted across the top of the colonnade as Maurice entered below. Nor did either of them notice the shape's distinct tail or sharp claws.

"You're not red," Maurice said, spotting a single perfect white rose among the hundreds of others, "but you'll do." Reaching into his pocket, he pulled out a small penknife. He placed the blade against the stem of the rose.

At that exact moment, Philippe whinnied and reared. Maurice whipped his head around. Seeing nothing, he shot Philippe a questioning glance and then turned back to the rose. The blade bit into the fragile stem. With a snip, the rose fell into Maurice's waiting hands.

"Those are *MINE!*"

The roar drowned out any other sound, including Maurice's thudding heart and Philippe's frantic neighs. Shaking, Maurice looked up just as a dark shape leapt down from the top of the colonnade. Maurice stumbled backward. The rose fell from his hand. His feet scrabbled for purchase on the slippery ground.

In front of him, the shadow took shape. It was vaguely human, but as it drew closer, Maurice saw that it was actually a gigantic furry creature. It walked on its hind legs and wore a flowing cloak and blue pants, but that was where the human similarities ended.

"You entered my home, ate my food," the creature said, dropping to all fours and circling Maurice. Raising one clawed paw, it pointed at the fallen rose. "And *this* is how I am repaid."

Maurice once again tried to move away, but he couldn't find his footing. Before he could even shout, the creature had grabbed him with two strong arms and lifted him high off the ground. "I know how to deal with thieves," he snarled. Then, with a growl, he turned and headed back into the castle.

Behind him, Philippe whinnied again in terror and bolted, charging through the castle gates and out into the woods beyond.

CHAPTER V

THE SUN HAD JUST RISEN OVER THE horizon as Belle made her way outside to give the chickens their morning meal. The birds chirped and a gentle breeze blew across the hillside. Combined with the beautiful, cloudless blue sky, it made for a picture-perfect morning.

And then Belle heard a familiar snort.

Turning her head, she was surprised to see Philippe standing by the gate to his paddock. His sides were heaving and soaked with sweat. The whites of his eyes showed as he shifted nervously on his feet.

"Philippe," Belle said, rushing over and letting the big horse into his paddock so he could drink. She patted him gently. "What are you doing here? Where is . . . ?" Her hand stilled. Then it began to shake as she saw the torn straps where the harness had once been attached. Her eyes grew even wider as she noticed the tattered reins. Something had happened to her father—something bad.

Not pausing to give her actions thought, Belle threw a saddle onto Philippe's back, tightened the girth, and put a new bridle over his head. She knew she was asking a lot of the horse, but he was the only one who knew where her father was. Mounting, she kicked the horse forward.

Belle knew that her father had gone into the woods. That much she was sure of; it was the route he always took. But as Philippe left the familiar countryside of the village and cantered through the thickening forest, her hopes grew dimmer. This part of the forest was huge. Finding one man among all of it seemed almost impossible. "Hurry, Philippe," she said as the horse veered around a tree that had been split in half. "Lead me to him."

The woods grew still thicker, the sky still darker, but Philippe plunged bravely ahead. Belle scanned the ground and sides of the small path. Suddenly, she spotted her father's cart. It was on the ground, tipped on its side. Her father's beautiful music boxes were strewn about, some broken beyond repair, others less damaged. But there was no sign of her father.

Nudging Philippe with her heels, she urged him on again. The horse cantered forward, seemingly familiar with the thin and winding path. Belle could only hope that was because it was the way he and her father had gone.

To her relief, a gate came into view a moment later. Beyond the thick iron bars, she saw a giant stone castle. Philippe whinnied. Her father had to be in there, somewhere. Belle just knew it. Quickly, she dismounted and patted Philippe. She whispered words of encouragement, leading him inside the gate, and then asked him to wait. She moved to go up the stone steps, then paused. Belle was not about to go running into the strange castle with no way to protect herself. Looking around, she spotted a thick branch that had fallen to the ground. Picking it up, she held it over her head, brandishing it like a club. *Then* she made her way up to the front doors.

Belle didn't even bother to knock. If her father was indeed inside somewhere, she didn't want to waste any time in finding him. Pushing open the doors, she found herself inside a massive foyer. A few candles hung on the walls, barely casting enough light to illuminate the space. Squaring her shoulders, Belle took a deep breath and walked farther into the castle.

As Belle made her way toward the grand staircase, her eyes adjusted to the dark. She heard muffled whispers, but she couldn't see anyone. Two voices rose and fell, and then she heard one phrase uttered clear as day: "But what if she's the one? The one who will break the spell?"

"Who said that?" Belle asked, whipping around and peering in the direction she thought the voices had come from.

Nothing.

"Who's there?"

Still nothing.

And then, from somewhere deep within the castle, Belle heard the unmistakable sound of someone coughing. *Papa.* It didn't matter who was whispering. She just needed to find her father. Grabbing a candelabrum from a nearby table, Belle began to climb the long staircase, following it up to its very top. When she reached the end of the labyrinthine stairs, she found herself in a tower, which, she noticed with increasing dread, was used as a prison. A grated iron door stood opposite the stairs. The latticework was so thick it was impossible to see through it clearly, but she could make out the shape of someone sitting inside.

"Papa?" Belle called out. "Is that you?"

"Belle?" Maurice answered in a muffled voice. "How did you find me?"

Belle raced across the dim tower and dropped to her knees in front of the door. A narrow opening allowed her just enough space to see her father. He was hunched over, his shoulders trembling. When their eyes met, she knew instantly he was not well. Setting the candelabrum down on the floor beside her, she reached through the opening. Her fingers closed around her father's. "Oh, Papa," she said, sadness tearing through her. "Your hands are ice. We need to get you home."

To her surprise, Maurice did not agree. "Belle, you must leave this place!" he said. When she ignored him and started to use the branch to hit the iron lock, he grew more and more agitated. "Stop! They'll hear you!"

Belle paused. "Who's 'they'?" she asked, cocking her head. She thought about the phantom voices she'd heard earlier. "Who did this to you?"

"No time to explain!" her father said. "You *must* go!"

Belle shook her head stubbornly. "I won't leave you!"

Her father stifled a groan. He had always loved his daughter's tenacity and spirit, but for once he just wanted her to do what he said. He couldn't stomach the idea of his sweet girl meeting the creature who had put him in that cell. "Belle, this castle is alive!" he said, trying to make her understand. "You must get away before he finds you!"

"'He'?" Belle repeated.

Before Maurice could open his mouth to respond, a roar filled the tower. Belle spun around, raising her branch high in the air. But it was no use. She couldn't see anything in the thick shadows. She could, however, hear a voice—a deep, rumbling voice that seemed to surround her, making her heart pound faster.

"Who are *you?*" the voice said. "How did you get in here?"

"I've come for my father," Belle said, trying to sound braver than she felt. "Release him."

The voice sounded closer as it hissed the next words: "Your father is a thief."

Belle recoiled as if she had been struck, fear turning into outrage. How dare the voice accuse her father like that? "Liar!" she shouted. Her father was a loving and kind man. He was a gentle man. He would never do anything like—

"He stole a rose!" the voice roared.

As Belle's head whipped back toward her father, her brown eyes locked with his. Guilt suddenly flooded through her as the reality of what must have happened hit her. "I asked for the rose," she said in barely a whisper.

"Belle . . ." Maurice said sadly, confirming what she knew to be true. Her father had taken the rose only because it was the one thing she had asked him to bring her. It was *her* fault he was in that cell—her fault entirely.

"Punish me, not him," Belle said, tearing her eyes away from her father and speaking to the invisible source of the voice.

"No!" Maurice shouted in anguish. "He means to keep me forever. Apparently, that's what happens around here when you pick a flower."

Belle frowned. "A life sentence for a rose?" she said to the shadows, hoping her father might be wrong.

"I received eternal damnation for one," came the voice out of the dark. "I'm merely locking him away." There was a pause, as though whoever the voice belonged to was distracted, thinking of some distant memory. And then the voice came again, colder than ever. "Now . . . do you still wish to take your father's place?"

Belle had had enough of talking to air. She wanted to see with whom she was bargaining for her life. "Come into the light," she demanded.

Behind her, her father murmured, "No," and shuffled back in his cell. But the voice did not answer. Belle reached down and grabbed the candelabrum that had been sitting by her father's cell. She lifted it. For one brief moment, the light blinded her. But when her eyes adjusted, Belle gasped.

Standing in front of her was a huge creature unlike any Belle had ever seen. Large horns rose out of his head, and his lower jaw jutted forward. His entire body was covered in golden-brown hair and thick muscles. It was hard for Belle to tell just how big the creature's front paws were, clenched in fists as they were, but his back paws were large and long, with sharp claws that flashed when the light hit them. The word *beast* flashed in her mind as she gazed at the creature. He was a thing of nightmares—the monster lurking in the fairy tales she had read as a child.

But when Belle lifted her eyes to meet the Beast's,

she was surprised by how human they looked—and how full of pain they seemed. Blue as the morning sky, they stared back at her, haunted. She felt a strange pang of what was almost sympathy for the giant creature. And then . . .

"*Choose!*" The Beast's lips curled back over sharp fangs as he snarled his demand.

All feelings but those of dread and disgust vanished. Belle looked back at her father, who pleaded with her not to do anything rash.

"But you'll die here," she said, knowing all too well it was true.

"*I SAID CHOOSE!*" the Beast snarled once again.

"No, Belle," Maurice said, trying to reason with his headstrong daughter. "I couldn't save your mother, but I can save you. Now go!" But his words lost their power as a coughing fit overtook him. The coughs racked his already weakened body and broke Belle's heart.

"All right, Papa. I'll leave," Belle said, trying to reassure Maurice and make him stop coughing. Then she turned to the Beast. "Open the door. I need a minute alone with him." She waited for the large creature to do something. He didn't. "Please?" Still he ignored her request. Anger flared in her chest once more, hot and fierce. "Are you so coldhearted that you won't allow a daughter to kiss her father good-bye? Forever can spare a minute!"

Belle's chest heaved as she waited for the Beast to respond. For one long tense moment, he just stared at her with cold, cruel eyes and she wondered if she had gone too far. He took a step toward her, his massive paw reaching out. She closed her eyes and braced herself for his retaliation.

She heard a clang. Opening her eyes, she saw that the Beast had opened the cell door. He gestured for her to enter. "When this door closes," he warned as she passed, "it will not open again."

Belle didn't hesitate. She rushed inside and embraced her father. "I'm so sorry, Papa," she sobbed. "I should have gone with you!"

Maurice put his hands on Belle's shoulders and gently pushed her back until they were eye to eye. "No, this was my fault," he said, shaking his head. He reached out and pinched her cheek the way he had done when she was a little girl. It had always reassured her then. Now it just made her sad. He went on, his voice choked with emotion. "Listen, Belle. Forget about me. I've had my life. . . ."

"Forget you?" Belle said in disbelief. "How could I ever? Everything I am is because of you."

Belle's words seemed to hit Maurice like a punch to the stomach. He looked at her as though seeing her for the first time—not the smart, sweet little girl he had raised on his own, but the brave, strong woman she had become. It all seemed too much for the older man. Tears flooded his eyes.

"Enough of this," the Beast said, his harsh voice stabbing into both father and daughter. "She must go."

Belle and Maurice clung to each other.

"Now!" The Beast's voice tore them apart.

"I love you, Belle," Maurice said. "Don't be afraid."

"I love you, Papa. I'm not afraid," Belle said, leaning

forward and gently kissing him on the cheek. As she did so, she maneuvered her body so her back was to the cell door, her hands on her father's shoulders. And then, in barely a whisper, she added, "And I will escape. I promise. . . ."

Before Maurice could stop her, Belle pivoted her body. The force swung her father through the door just as the Beast slammed it shut. Falling to the ground, Maurice cried out as the reality of what his daughter had just sacrificed became clear.

It seemed to hit the Beast at the same moment. And while it obviously devastated Maurice, the Beast appeared confused. "You took his place?" he asked Belle. "Why?"

"He is my father," she answered without hesitation.

"He's a fool," the Beast retorted. "And so are you." Without another word, he grabbed Maurice by the shirt and began to drag him away.

Belle stifled the sob that threatened to escape her throat. She watched silently through the gate as her father and the Beast disappeared down the stairs. She waited until she was sure she was alone, and only when silence had descended on the tower did she finally slump to the ground. As the tears fell, colder and harsher than the snow that had once again begun to fall outside, one thought echoed through her mind: what was to become of her?

CHAPTER VI

THE BEAST WAS TIRED—TIRED AND perplexed. He was still not sure how it happened that he now held a beautiful young woman prisoner while her father, the real thief, was making his way back toward the comfort of his home. He shook his head. No, it did not make sense.

But then again, he thought as he pushed open the castle's front door, nothing had made sense in his life in a long, long time.

Storming inside the foyer, the Beast nearly collided with Lumiere and Cogsworth. The candelabrum and clock had been waiting anxiously for him to return. "Master," Lumiere began, "since the girl is going to be with us for quite some time—"

"And I hope 'forever' was an exaggeration," Cogsworth said, his tone every bit as flat and polished as expected of a majordomo. "We don't have the staff for that kind of extended stay. . . ." His voice trailed off as the Beast turned and glared at him.

Not intimidated, Lumiere forged on. "Whether it's for a day or a lifetime," he said smoothly, "you might want to offer her a more comfortable room."

"This whole castle is a prison," the Beast said harshly. As he spoke, Chapeau, the coatrack, tried to take the Beast's cloak. The Beast brushed him off and continued walking toward the grand staircase. Over his shoulder, he added, "What difference does a bed make?" Not waiting for an answer, he disappeared into the shadows.

Cogsworth waited to speak until he was sure his master couldn't hear him, and even then, he did so under his breath. "Yes. It's a prison thanks to you, Sire. I just love being a clock." He sighed bitterly. As head of the Beast's household, Cogsworth knew he was supposed to be the picture of respect at all times. But sometimes that was difficult. Sometimes it was hard to forget that he and every other member of the staff were in the state they were in because of the master they still had to serve. "I knew he wouldn't say yes."

"But technically . . . he didn't say no," Lumiere pointed out. Flashing Cogsworth a sly smile, the candelabrum headed toward the stairs that led to the prison tower.

Behind him, Cogsworth remained still. He knew what Lumiere had in mind. The romantic footman was as easy to read as a book. The candelabrum wanted to free the girl and put her somewhere more noticeable—in the hopes that she might be the one who could break the curse they were all under, the curse that had remained unbroken for those long years because of one obvious fact: the Beast was a beast, both literally and figuratively. And the curse the Enchantress had placed on them required someone to love him despite that.

Cogsworth sighed. He knew his friend was well intentioned. But Cogsworth was a realist. No matter where the girl laid her head, she would not love the Beast. And if Lumiere got his way and brought her out of the prison, it would only make the master furious. Cogsworth began waddling toward the stairs. He was going to have to stop Lumiere before the candelabrum did something they would all regret.

But Lumiere had already opened the cell door. "Forgive my intrusion, mademoiselle," he said into the darkness, "but the master has sent me to escort you to your room."

Belle was sitting on the floor, her cheeks stained with tears. Hearing Lumiere's voice, she stood. "My room?" she said, sounding confused. "But I thought—"

"You thought wrong," Lumiere replied. "He is a beast. Not a monster."

A moment later, Belle appeared in the cell doorway, brandishing a stool over her head. She looked around for the source of the voice she had heard.

"*Allô*," Lumiere said.

Looking down, Belle saw Lumiere waving at her with one of his candlesticks. She screamed. Then, as if he were a mouse that had surprised her in the pantry,

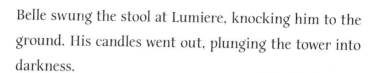

Belle swung the stool at Lumiere, knocking him to the ground. His candles went out, plunging the tower into darkness.

One by one, the three candles that made up the candelabrum relit. As Belle watched, the flickers of light illuminated two eyes and a mouth in the elaborate design of the metal. "What *are* you?" she finally asked.

"I am Lumiere," the candelabrum replied, flashing Belle what could only be called a rakish smile.

"And you can talk," Belle observed.

Suddenly, Cogsworth waddled into the tower. He was out of breath from the long climb, and for a moment he just stood there, his little clock chest heaving. "Of course he can talk," he finally said. "How else is he supposed to communicate?" Turning, he put his hands on his hips and glared at Lumiere. "As head of the household, I demand to know what you are doing."

"It is better to ask for forgiveness than permission," Lumiere replied cryptically.

As the duo bickered, Belle inched her way back into

the cell. She reappeared a moment later with a pitcher of water in her hands. Seeing the potentially harmful weapon, Lumiere held up a golden arm. "*Un moment, mademoiselle . . .*" he said. Then he pulled Cogsworth aside. He lowered his voice to a whisper. "If we don't break the curse before the last petal falls, we will never be human again. What do you want to be for the rest of your life, Cogsworth—a man or a mantel clock?"

Cogsworth frowned. Lumiere was right. Still . . . "If he catches us . . ."

"We will be quiet," Lumiere promised. He looked at Cogsworth with an expression bordering on desperate. Finally, the clock gave the slightest of nods. Lumiere didn't wait. Turning, he looked back at Belle. "Ready, miss?" he asked, bowing and pointing one of his candles toward the tower's exit.

Belle looked back and forth between the candelabrum and the clock. Then she looked at the cell. While neither option was exactly comforting, following the talking household objects at least meant getting out of a cell. Taking a deep breath, she leaned down, picked up Lumiere, and followed Cogsworth out of the tower.

As the trio made their way across a long stone walkway, Belle's eyes darted back and forth. But no matter where she looked, she could not make out an escape route of any kind. The woods that stretched out behind the castle were vast—and a bit intimidating.

Although, she thought as she looked down at her companions, the castle wasn't exactly making her feel warm or fuzzy. She eyed Lumiere and Cogsworth and, for the umpteenth time, resisted the urge to turn Lumiere upside down and look for the strings that had to be making him move. And once again, she stopped herself from peering over her shoulder to try to spot the ventriloquist she knew must be lurking somewhere nearby, giving voice to two objects that, in her experience, were usually inanimate. Both times, she stopped herself because she knew it would do no good. Somehow, the candelabrum and clock were *alive*.

"You must forgive first impressions," Lumiere said, as if sensing her thoughts. "I hope you are not too startled."

"Startled?" Belle repeated with a sarcastic laugh. "Why would I be startled? I'm talking to a candle."

Lumiere looked aghast. "Candel-a-bra," he corrected, enunciating each syllable. "Enormous difference. But we do hope you enjoy your stay here. The castle is your home now, so feel free to go anywhere you like—"

"Except the West Wing."

In unison, Belle and Lumiere turned to look at the clock. But while Lumiere was shooting him a barely veiled "Would you please shut your mouth?" look, Belle stared at him with evident curiosity. She opened her mouth to ask where the forbidden West Wing might be but was stopped by Cogsworth trying to cover his tracks.

"Which we do not have," he added.

It was too late. Belle wanted to know more. "Why?" she asked. "What's in the West Wing?"

"Uh . . ." Lumiere stammered, the flames on his candles flickering nervously. "Nothing. Storage space."

Belle raised an eyebrow, clearly not buying the candelabrum's explanation. She raised her arm so that Lumiere's light illuminated a nearby curved stone window, displaying a tower that rose out of the western portion of the castle. As she did so, the moon appeared over the horizon, casting an eerie light on the tower. Belle could have sworn she saw the Beast's shadow in the white light and heard an anguished cry. Shivering, she lowered Lumiere.

"This way, please," the candelabrum said, eager to move them along.

With one last glance over her shoulder, Belle sighed and once again followed Cogsworth as he waddled down one hallway and along another. Finally, he came to a stop in front of a large door.

"Welcome to your new home," Lumiere said in a grandiose tone.

Belle's hand hovered over the doorknob. A part of

her wanted to turn the knob. Another part of her was terrified to do so. She had no idea what to expect. If the room was anything like the rest of the castle, with its layers of dust and oppressive sad portraits and decaying furniture, she was going to have to insist they bring her back to the tower.

Taking a deep breath, she turned the knob and pushed open the door. The light from Lumiere's three candles filled the space. Belle gasped. She was looking into what appeared to be a gorgeous bedroom—far more elegant than any she had ever seen in real life or imagined in her stories.

As if in a dream, she slowly walked inside, her eyes feasting on every perfect detail of the room. There was a large white-and-gold-painted armoire along one wall, and along another wall a beautiful writing desk had been placed. A chair, covered in rich velvet, was tucked underneath it, and a stack of crisp white paper was placed on one side. Opposite a set of huge picture windows covered by thick satin drapes was an enormous canopy bed that took up nearly a third of the room. And tucked in a corner, delicate and sweet, was a dressing table with a mirror framed in gold. Even the ceiling of the room was breathtaking. White clouds had been painted in a perfect blue sky, the detail so real Belle could have sworn she saw the clouds move.

"It's . . . beautiful," she finally said when she realized Lumiere and Cogsworth were staring at her, waiting for a response.

Lumiere smiled broadly while Cogsworth nodded, his pleasure more contained. "Of course. Master wanted you to have the finest room in the castle," Lumiere said, making his way to the bed and leaping onto it. A cloud of dust rose into the air. "Oh, dear! We weren't expecting guests."

As if on cue, a feather duster swooped into the room. Belle's eyes widened as the feather duster quickly moved from surface to surface, sweeping until everything shined. Stopping, she bowed in Belle's direction. "*Enchanté*, mademoiselle! Don't worry, I'll have this room spotless in no time," she said before turning and jumping into the arms of Lumiere. "This plan of yours is . . . dangerous," she said, giggling.

Belle stifled her own giggle as Lumiere waggled his eyebrows and replied, "I would risk anything to kiss you again, Plumette. . . ." He leaned closer and puckered his lips.

Plumette stopped him. "No, my love," she said, her voice serious. "I've been burned by you before. We must be strong."

"How can I be strong when you make me so weak?" Lumiere replied.

Belle averted her eyes from the romantic pair and turned her attention toward other items in the room. "Is everything here alive?" she asked, picking up a brush. "Hello, what's *your* name?"

Cogsworth looked at Belle and shook his head. "Um . . . that's a hairbrush," he said as though pointing out the obvious.

Belle opened her mouth to ask just what the rules were for enchanted objects when, suddenly, a loud snore sounded behind her. Turning, she yelped as the large armoire's drawers opened and shut by themselves in time with the snoring.

"Do not be alarmed, mademoiselle," Lumiere said calmly. "This is just your wardrobe. Meet Madame de Garderobe, a great singer."

The armoire let out a long, loud yawn.

"A better sleeper," Cogsworth added as he walked over and nudged the wardrobe.

With a grunt, Garderobe awoke. Blinking the sleep out of her eyes, she gave a surprised little shout when she noticed her audience. "Cogsworth!" she exclaimed in an overly dramatic manner. "You officious alarm clock. A diva needs her beauty rest!"

Cogsworth's springs tightened at the insult and his mouth opened, ready with a sharp rebuke. But Lumiere didn't give him the chance. He jumped in before the clock could say a word. "Of course you do, madame," he said in his most soothing voice. "Forgive us, but we have someone for you to dress."

Spotting Belle for the first time, Garderobe emitted

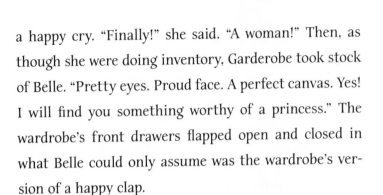

a happy cry. "Finally!" she said. "A woman!" Then, as though she were doing inventory, Garderobe took stock of Belle. "Pretty eyes. Proud face. A perfect canvas. Yes! I will find you something worthy of a princess." The wardrobe's front drawers flapped open and closed in what Belle could only assume was the wardrobe's version of a happy clap.

"But I'm not a princess," Belle said.

"Nonsense!" Garderobe said, brushing off Belle's protest. "Now, let's see what I've got in my drawers." Opening up the top one, she shouted as a few moths flew out. "How embarrassing!" she said.

To Belle's surprise, both sides of the armoire went from white to a soft shade of pink. The armoire was blushing!

Before Belle could ask how such a thing was possible—how *any* of it was possible, for that matter—Garderobe began to pull things helter-skelter out of her drawers and off hangers. A large hoopskirt went over Belle's head, followed by at least four different dresses cut right then and there by the wardrobe to be used as fabric. Belle was turned and twisted as Garderobe assembled an outfit.

When the wardrobe paused to take a breath, Belle snuck a peek at her reflection in the mirror across the room. To her horror, she saw the wardrobe had indeed created something from what she had in her drawers. But the result was the most garish ensemble Belle had ever seen. It seemed to swallow her up in shades of blue, pink, and yellow. Catching Lumiere's eye, Belle saw that the candelabrum was equally mortified. But both he and Cogsworth backed toward the door. They knew not to mess with Garderobe when she was in the middle of a creation.

"Anyway," Lumiere said, "if you have further needs, the staff will attend to them. We are at your service. Au revoir!" Then, with a deep bow, he grabbed Cogsworth and slipped out of the room. Plumette followed close behind. A moment later, the door closed, leaving Belle alone with Garderobe.

Belle didn't hesitate. She had a feeling that if she was ever going to get answers, the diva armoire was going to be the one to give them to her. Turning to Garderobe, she asked the question she had wanted to ask ever since Lumiere had revealed himself to her. "How did you get here?"

As she suspected, Garderobe's eyes lit up at the chance to gossip. Leaning her large frame over the bed, she lowered her voice to a conspiratorial whisper. "All it takes is a stormy night and one spoiled little prince . . ." But Garderobe's voice faded into soft snores as sleep overcame her.

Belle sighed. It looked like she wasn't going to be getting answers after all. At least not anytime soon. Belle quickly slipped out of the disaster of a dress. Then she turned and looked around the room. She was alone, her only guardian fast asleep. Now was the time for her to try to make her escape. The only question was, how?

CHAPTER VII

GASTON STILL COULDN'T BELIEVE IT. He had been rejected. Coldly, flatly, completely rejected. As he sat in *his* favorite chair in *his* favorite spot in the town tavern—right below the wall featuring all the antlers and trophies *he* had won—Gaston could not shake the bad feeling in the pit of his stomach. Even LeFou, sitting by his side, telling him how fantastic he was, could not break through the sorrow he felt.

"Picture it, LeFou," Gaston said, taking a big swallow from his drink. He waved his hand in front of him. "A rustic cabin. My latest kill roasting on the fire. Adorable children running around us while my love rubs my tired feet."

"Ooh! What's roasting on the fire?" LeFou said, ever

the captive and willing audience. "It's the minor details that really paint the picture."

Gaston shot the smaller man a look for interrupting his monologue. "But what does Belle say?" he asked, the picture painted clearly enough in his own mind. " 'I will *never* marry you, Gaston.' " He slammed down his drink in anger.

"There *are* other girls," LeFou pointed out. He nodded over his shoulder at a group of such girls. Gaston barely gave them a glance, but it was enough to send them into fits of giggles.

LeFou was right. Gaston could have the pick of any of the girls in the village—or the next village. Or any village, for that matter. But that wasn't the point. He didn't want any of those girls. "A great hunter doesn't waste his time on rabbits," he finally said. His words echoed through the tavern, causing the girls' flirtatious smiles to fade on their faces.

Slumping down in his chair, Gaston absently played with a piece of string hanging from the fraying cushion. Vaguely, he heard LeFou trying to cheer him up, but he barely paid attention. LeFou's arguments—that he was the bravest, strongest, most admired man in the village—were tired. Gaston had heard them all before. And, of course, he knew they were all true. He was exceptional. He was the town hero, the best hunter there was; he was even good at decoration—antlers made a room, in his opinion—and there was no doubt in anyone's mind he was the largest and most handsome of men.

But what does it matter whether all those things are true, Gaston thought, *if Belle doesn't believe it?*

Just then, the door to the tavern flew open. Maurice stood in the doorway. His eyes were wild and his clothing was torn. He grabbed on to the doorjamb as a cough racked his body. "Help!" he said when the coughing had subsided. "Somebody help me! We have to go . . . not a minute to lose . . ."

As he spoke, Maurice moved into the tavern, seeking out the warmth of the fire that roared in the hearth.

Seeing how disheveled the man was, the tavern keeper tried to calm him. "Whoa, whoa, whoa," he said. "Slow down, Maurice."

Maurice shook his head. "He's got Belle . . . locked in a dungeon!"

Gaston sat up straighter, his interest piqued.

"Who's got her?" the tavern keeper asked.

"A beast!" Maurice answered. "A horrible, monstrous beast!"

Shocked by the man's words, the whole inn went silent—for a moment. And then Jean the potter held up his mug and smiled. "What are you putting in this stuff?" he asked, breaking the silence.

The tavern keeper shook his head. "Don't look at me," he retorted. "He just got here."

Down at the other end of the counter, a vagrant who *hadn't* just gotten there looked up. The man was even more disheveled than Maurice and his eyes were cloudy, his cheeks weathered. He glanced at Maurice and nodded, as though he and Maurice were in on it together. "What they don't tell you is there used to be a castle and we don't remember any of it!" he said.

Instantly, the tavern filled with laughter.

"No!" Maurice protested. "He could be right! My daughter's life is in danger, why do you laugh? This isn't a joke! His castle is hidden in the woods. It's already winter there!"

"Winter in June?" Jean said, laughing. "Crazy old Maurice."

"Please listen!" Maurice begged, looking around the room at the dispassionate faces. "The Beast is real. Will no one help me?"

Sitting in his chair, Gaston stayed silent. Belle's father was an odd man. He always had been. But as the man continued to beg, an idea began to form in the back of Gaston's mind. An idea that could get him exactly what he wanted and make him look like the hero—again.

Quickly, Gaston got to his feet. "I'll help you, Maurice," he said grandly.

"You will?" LeFou asked, confused by his friend's sudden generosity.

Gaston turned and winked at LeFou and mouthed, *Just watch.* Then he addressed the room. "Everyone! Stop making fun of this man at once!" Instantly, the laughter died. He nodded. He really *was* the most respected man in town.

Maurice rushed over and fell to his knees. "Thank you, Captain," he said gratefully. "Thank you."

"Don't thank me, Maurice," Gaston said, pulling the old man to his feet. "Lead us to the Beast."

Still mumbling his thanks, Maurice headed out of the tavern. Gaston and LeFou exchanged looks as they followed him. The other patrons, seeing their beloved Gaston on a mission, followed, as well. Soon there was a parade making its way through the village. The commotion woke still others, who eagerly joined in, despite not knowing what was going on.

"I see what you're doing," LeFou said in a whisper as they walked.

Gaston nodded. He had known LeFou would figure

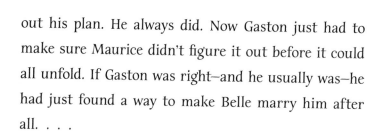

out his plan. He always did. Now Gaston just had to make sure Maurice didn't figure it out before it could all unfold. If Gaston was right—and he usually was—he had just found a way to make Belle marry him after all. . . .

Inside the Beast's castle, things were a bit calmer than they were back in the village . . . but not by much. Ever since Belle's arrival, the staff had been in a full-blown tizzy. It wasn't very often they had a guest in the castle. In fact, they hadn't had a guest in the castle since that fateful night. Determined to make Belle feel at home—in the hopes that perhaps one day the castle could *be* her home—every member of the household was doing some part to make everything perfect, starting with dinner.

The kitchen staff hurried about excitedly. Headed by Mrs. Potts—a no-nonsense teapot with a heart of gold—they were putting together an elaborate meal for Belle and their master.

Sitting atop her tea service trolley, Mrs. Potts

watched with pleasure as plates and serving ware that had long since gone unused came out of their drawers and cupboards. Beside her, her son, Chip, hopped up and down with excitement. "Mama," the little teacup said, "there's a girl in the castle!"

"Yes, Chip," Mrs. Potts said gently. "We know."

"Is she pretty? Is she nice?" Chip asked, jumping on his saucer and using it to zip around his mother. "What kind of tea does she like? Herbal? Oolong? Chamomile?"

"We'll find out soon enough," Mrs. Potts said. "Now slow down before you break your handle!"

At that moment, Lumiere and Cogsworth entered. The candelabrum quickly made his way over to Cuisinier, the large stove—complete with cooktop, range, vent hood, and ovens—in the middle of the kitchen. "This is your night," Lumiere said seriously. "We are counting on you, Monsieur Cuisinier."

The stove puffed up proudly. "Finally!" he said. His voice sounded rusty, as though it had not been used in quite some time. "A chance to cook again. Do you know what it's been like pleasing a beast's palate? 'Stag tartare with the antlers on' every single day! Who eats chicken for dessert, I ask you? Who?" As he stopped to take a breath, Cuisinier's sides heaved with indignation.

Knowing it was best to appease the rather temperamental stove, Lumiere nodded sympathetically. "Tonight, you make a soufflé!"

"LUMIERE!"

The Beast's roar echoed in the kitchen—it seemed the master was on his way. Instantly, Lumiere's flames dimmed. Cogsworth shook. They both knew the Beast was not pleased.

"Just . . . let me do the talking," Lumiere said to the majordomo. While Cogsworth was very good at running a household—and telling time—he was terrible at knowing the right thing to say. He had been known, on more than one occasion, to try to escape blame at any cost. It would be best for all those involved if Lumiere was the one to deal with the Beast. At least, he hoped it would be.

A moment later, the doors to the kitchen burst open

and the Beast appeared. His chest was heaving and his blue eyes were stormy as he took in the assembled staff. He sniffed the air, which was filled with the delicious smells of cooking, and his eyes grew even stormier. "You are making her dinner?" he growled.

"We thought you might appreciate the company," Lumiere replied in his most politic voice. He opened his mouth to explain the benefits of dining with another when Cogsworth jumped in. Lumiere shot him a look, begging him to stay silent, but the clock would not be stopped.

"Master," Cogsworth said, trying to cover his own wheels and pins, "I can assure you that I had no part in this hopeless plan. Preparing a dinner, designing a gown for her, giving her a suite in the East Wing—"

"You gave her a bedroom?" The Beast's shout had enough force to blow out Lumiere's candles.

Cogsworth backpedaled. "I . . . I . . . well," he stammered. "You said . . . um . . . that the whole castle was a prison, so what difference would a bed make . . ."

Seeing his friend struggle, Lumiere jumped in. "That is true, master," he pointed out. "And if the girl is the one who can break the spell, maybe you can start by using dinner to charm her." He turned and threw his friend a bone. "Good plan, Cogsworth."

The Beast narrowed his eyes. Then he began to pace back and forth. Finally, he looked at Lumiere and Cogsworth. "The idea is ridiculous," he said. "*Charm* the prisoner?"

"You must *try*, master," Lumiere said. He took a deep breath. He knew that what he was about to say was not something the master wanted to hear. But nevertheless, it needed to be said. "With every passing day, we become less human."

Behind him, the staff piped up, adding their own encouragement. He heard someone say "You can do it," and another member of the staff added, "Please." In their voices, Lumiere heard the same desperation he felt. Their master's fate was their fate—yet only the Beast could change it.

"She's the daughter of a common thief," the Beast

pointed out, his staff's pleas falling on deaf ears. "What kind of person do you think that makes her?"

Mrs. Potts, who had been silent up until that point, finally spoke up. "Oh, you can't judge people by who their father is, now can you?"

She didn't need to say more; her loaded statement was clear enough. All around her, the staff cringed, prepared for the master to retaliate. But to their surprise, he didn't. He paused for a moment, his eyes locked on Mrs. Potts. She knew, more than many, just how deep a wound the master's father had left on him.

Finally, with a resigned grunt, the Beast turned and left the kitchen. Lumiere, Cogsworth, and Mrs. Potts exchanged glances. And then they rushed after him, knowing he couldn't be left to his own devices to ask the girl to dinner.

CHAPTER VIII

THE BEAST STOOD IN FRONT OF THE door to the bedroom that now, against his wishes, belonged to Belle. Beside him, his key staff waited, ready to help if necessary. He glared at them, and then, raising one big paw, he knocked. Twice.

"You will join me for dinner!" he said, not waiting for a response from Belle. "That's not a request!"

On her serving trolley, Mrs. Potts gave a small cough. "Gently, master," she advised. "Remember, the girl lost her father and her freedom in one day."

"Yes," Lumiere agreed. "The poor thing is probably in there scared to death."

The Beast sighed. He was getting rather tired of the sudden onslaught of advice. Still, he knocked again.

This time, there came an answer. "Just a minute." Belle's voice was muffled through the thick door.

"You see!" Lumiere said happily. "There she is! Now, master, remember, be gentle . . ."

"Kind . . ." added Mrs. Potts.

"Charming!" Plumette chirped.

"And when she opens the door," Lumiere finished, "give her a dashing, debonair smile. Come, come–show me the smile."

Show him the smile? the Beast repeated to himself. Had Lumiere lost his mind? He hadn't smiled in years. There had been no reason to. He started to point that out, but a look from Mrs. Potts stopped him. Reluctantly, he tensed the muscles in his face, pulling his lips back over his teeth.

In unison, his staff took a horrified step back.

"Eh, less teeth," Lumiere suggested.

The Beast didn't need a mirror to know that his first attempt at a smile had resulted in the most hideous grin anyone had ever seen. He tried again.

"More teeth?" Plumette said.

The Beast sighed. Still hideous, he supposed. Once more, he adjusted his smile.

"*Different* teeth?" Cogsworth advised.

"How about no teeth?" Mrs. Potts added.

The Beast flashed a warning look. He had had enough. The staff wanted him to ask Belle to dinner. He would ask her to dinner. He would *not*, however, spend any more time trying to smile. Knocking once more, he tried again: "Will you join me for dinner?"

This time, Belle's response was much swifter. "You've taken me prisoner and now you're asking me to dine with you?" Her voice sounded closer now, as though she were right on the other side of the door. "Are you mad?"

As Belle's words registered with the Beast, his expression grew dark. His paws clenched at his sides and his lips pulled up in a snarl.

"Calm yourself, master," Mrs. Potts said in her most reassuring tone. She knew the Beast was only moments away from losing his temper.

"But she is infuriating," the Beast replied through clenched teeth. "Difficult."

Mrs. Potts tried not to smile at the irony of her

master's calling Belle difficult. She attempted to reason with him instead. "So, you be *easy*," she said.

Taking a deep breath, the Beast prepared to try once more. His body shook with the effort and his jaw clenched fiercely, but he managed to speak in a tone that was mostly nice. "It would give me great pleasure if you would join me for dinner."

Belle's response was immediate. "It would give *me* great pleasure," she said through the door, "if you would go away."

That was the final straw. The Beast's eyebrows twitched. His tail thrashed. His claws flashed, and then, as the staff backed away, he lifted his paw and banged on the door with all his strength. The hallway shook.

"I told you to come to dinner!" he snarled, all nicety gone.

Belle did not back down. She banged on the other side of the door. "And I told you *no*! I'd starve before I ever ate a meal with you!"

"Be my guest," the Beast shouted back. "Go ahead and *starve*!" Turning, he glared at his staff. They were the ones who had gotten him into this mess in the first place. "If she doesn't eat with me, then she doesn't eat at all!"

"Master, no!" Lumiere protested. "Show her the real you."

"This *is* the real me," the Beast said. Without another word, he whipped around and headed toward his rooms. Behind him, he could hear the staff muttering to themselves, their voices disappointed. But he didn't care. What had they expected to happen? For Belle to swoon at the idea of eating dinner with *him*? A *beast*? They were fools if they thought that would happen. And he had been a fool to try.

Pushing open the door to the West Wing, he stalked over to a small table by the window. On top of it were a hand mirror and a glass jar, which held a single red rose that hung, enchanted, in its center. Picking up the mirror, the Beast gave a single command. "Show me the girl!"

Magic whirled and the mirror's glass slowly shifted and swirled until it revealed Belle. She sat, her back against the door of her room and a look of dread on her face.

Slowly, he put the mirror down. Belle was scared because of him, because of the beast he was—the beast he might very well always be. His eyes locked on the enchanted rose and he sighed, watching as another petal fell to the table. It was only a matter of time now before the last petal fell, and when that happened . . . The Beast shuddered and lowered his head. When that happened, all hope would be lost. And if Belle's reaction was any indication, he had just blown one of his few chances to put an end to the curse.

I have to get out of here, Belle thought as she pushed herself to her feet. The Beast was a monster. His behavior just then had proven that beyond a doubt. If she didn't get away now, she would most likely be stuck with him forever. She shuddered at the horrifying thought.

Walking over to the window, she looked out. After she had been left alone with a narcoleptic wardrobe as her only guardian, she had wasted no time in putting an escape plan into action. Ripping apart the hideous dress Garderobe had made her, she had used the fabric to create a makeshift rope. It now hung out the window, the end dangling about twenty feet from the ground. It wasn't perfect, but it would do.

She had just taken a deep breath and picked up the rope when . . . *Knock! Knock! Knock!*

"I told you to go away!" she shouted over her shoulder.

To her surprise, it was not the Beast's deep and grumbling voice that answered. Instead, the voice that replied was gentle, kind, and polished. "Don't worry, dear," it said. "It's not the master. It's Mrs. Potts." A moment later, the door swung open and a serving trolley rolled inside. Placed on top were a beautifully painted teapot and a teacup with the same design on its side. The pot, Belle had to assume, was Mrs. Potts.

Quickly, Belle tried to block the rope that hung behind her. But Mrs. Potts had spotted the escape route the moment she had entered the room. It hadn't surprised her. Belle seemed like a clever girl, and the master had given her no reason to feel welcome. Still, Mrs. Potts wasn't going to let the girl just leave—not if she could help it. And having lived with a stubborn individual for quite some time, she knew that sometimes the best way to make people do what they didn't want to do was to give them the chance to do it on their own terms.

"It's a very long journey, my lamb," Mrs. Potts said sweetly. "Let me fix you up before you go. I have found in my experience that most troubles seem less troubling after a bracing cup o' tea. Isn't that right, Madame de Garderobe?" Mrs. Potts turned and addressed the armoire, who was still fast asleep. "Madame! Wake up!"

With a jolt, Garderobe awoke. "What?" she asked, sounding sleepy and confused. "I fell asleep again?"

"Madame used to sleep eight hours a day," the small teacup piped up. "Now she sleeps twenty-three."

"That'll do, Chip," Mrs. Potts warned. "It's not polite to discuss a lady's habits."

But Chip, as Belle now knew him, had given her pause. And since she had gotten no answers from Garderobe earlier, she decided to try again. "What happened here?" she asked. "Is this an enchantment? A curse?" That could be the only logical explanation for the castle's oddities, in Belle's opinion. She had read many a story about such things, but she had never thought they could be *real*.

"She guessed it, Mama," Chip said, lisping in his little voice through the chip in the front of his cup. "She's smart."

As he spoke, his mother hopped over and filled him with tea. Then she nudged him toward Belle. "Slowly now, Chip," she warned. "Don't spill tea. Or secrets."

Belle smiled despite herself as she picked up Chip. He was so obviously a little boy, yet somehow he was trapped in the shape of a cup. *How sad it must be*, Belle thought, *to not have the ability to do little-boy things.*

As if sensing what she was thinking, Chip asked, "Want to see me do a trick?" Belle nodded, and Chip took a deep breath. Then he started to blow bubbles. The tea splish-splashed inside his cup, making Belle laugh. The sound echoed nicely through the room, and Mrs. Potts smiled.

"That was a very brave thing you did for your father, dear," she remarked.

"We all think so," Garderobe said, nodding in agreement.

Belle's smile faded at the mention of her father. "I'm so worried about him," she said softly. "He's never been alone."

"Cheer up, my poppet," Mrs. Potts said, trying to get back some of the earlier levity. "Things will turn out in the end. You'll see. You'll feel a lot better after dinner."

Belle looked at the teapot and cocked her head. "But he said, 'If she doesn't eat with me, she doesn't eat at all.'" She had dropped her voice and tried to make it sound as scary and mean as possible. Mrs. Potts held in a sigh. The master really had made a bad impression on the poor girl.

"People say a lot of things in anger," she said. "It is our choice whether or not to listen." As she spoke, she turned the serving trolley toward the door and began to leave. Turning to look back at Belle, Mrs. Potts smiled. "Coming, poppety?"

Belle watched as the teapot disappeared out the door. Her stomach rumbled. *Fine,* she thought, *I'll go have dinner. But just this one meal. Then I am leaving . . . once and for all.*

The kitchen staff was ready. Lumiere had seen to it as soon as Mrs. Potts had told him she was going to speak with Belle. He knew it was only a matter of time before the kind teapot convinced Belle to come down for a quick bite.

But Lumiere had no intention of this being any small, quick bite. *This* meal was going to be one Belle would remember forever. It was going to involve the tastiest of hors d'oeuvres, the most delicious of entrees, the most delightful of drinks, and, of course, the most decadent of desserts. By the time Belle put her fork down, she would never want to leave. At least, that was what Lumiere *hoped*.

Bursting into the kitchen, he clasped two of his candles together. "They're coming!" he said excitedly. "Final checks, everyone, tout de suite!" With pleasure, he watched as every member of the kitchen staff sprang into action. They all knew as well as he how important this dinner was.

All of them, that is, except apparently Cogsworth.

"No, you don't!" the clock said, shuffling into the middle of the fray. He folded his two little arms across his gears. "If the master finds out you violated his orders and fed her, he will blame me."

Lumiere turned and stared at his friend. Then he sighed. How could Cogsworth be thinking of himself at a time like this? Making his way over, he nodded. "Yes," he said, his tone teasing but his intent serious. "I will make sure of it. But did you see her stand up to him? I am telling you, this girl is the one! They *must* fall in love if we are to be human again, and they can't fall in love if she stays in her room."

"You know she will never love him," Cogsworth said softly.

"A broken clock is right two times a day, my friend," Lumiere replied, refusing to let the stodgy majordomo get him down, "and this is not one of those times. We *must* try."

Turning away from Cogsworth, he moved over to Cuisinier. Pots and pans bubbled and steamed on the stove, filling the air with a tantalizing smell. Behind him, Lumiere could feel Cogsworth's eyes on him, and he knew that the majordomo was struggling. Lumiere didn't blame him. He was right. The master would think this was all Cogsworth's doing if he found out. But they had no other choice. It wasn't every day a girl happened upon the enchanted castle—and a girl with the strength to stand up to the master, at that. *No,* Lumiere thought, shaking his head and straightening his candles with resolve. This dinner was going to happen—with or without Cogsworth's blessing.

Finally, the clock sighed. Lumiere waited.

"At least keep it down," Cogsworth said, his voice soft.

A smile spread across Lumiere's face. But he wiped it away before turning to his friend and nodding. "Of course, of course," he said. "But what is dinner without a little . . . music?"

"Music?" Cogsworth cried, his voice no longer quiet. He began shaking his head.

But it was too late. Lumiere was already guiding a harpsichord into the dining room. "Maestro Cadenza," he said as he set him up in a corner of the room, "your wife is upstairs sleeping more and more each day. She is counting on you to help the master and this girl fall in love."

With a flourish, the harpsichord played a scale, grimacing when one of the notes fell flat. "Then I shall play through the pain," he said bravely.

At that moment, Mrs. Potts led Belle into the dining room. The girl looked around, awed by the elaborate spread set out on the table, but clearly still hesitant to be there. Lumiere saw the uneasiness in her eyes, and his resolve to make her comfortable grew stronger. He gave the staff one last knowing look, and then, with a flourish, he leapt onto the table.

"*Ma chère*, mademoiselle," he began as a beam of moonlight streamed through the window, making it appear as though the candelabrum were in the spotlight. He bowed. "It is with deepest pride and greatest pleasure that we welcome you tonight. We invite you to relax"—he nodded and the chair behind Belle moved in so that she sat, with a little squeak of surprise, and was pushed in to the table—"while we proudly present . . . your dinner."

At first Belle sat with her hands on her lap as Lumiere guided her, course by course, through her meal. But as she listened to him describe the food and watched as the enchanted silverware and dishware made a show and dance, she began to relax. Her hands unclenched the napkin she was holding and her foot tapped to the rhythm of the harpsichord. By the time Lumiere referred to the "gray stuff" as delicious, Belle

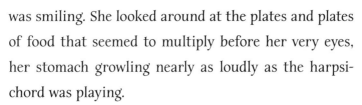

was smiling. She looked around at the plates and plates of food that seemed to multiply before her very eyes, her stomach growling nearly as loudly as the harpsichord was playing.

While Lumiere and the other staff continued to entertain her, Belle proceeded to eat to her heart's content. She tasted beef ragout and cheese soufflé. She dipped a freshly baked baguette in foie gras and sighed with pleasure as the food melted on her tongue. Each dish presented was better than the last, and every time Belle thought she wouldn't be able to eat a bite more, a platter presented itself and she found room.

Throughout it all, the music played, as wonderful as the food itself. By the time the meal was over, Belle was enchanted. It was hard not to be when all the servants seemed so happy to have her there, so pleased to be working. It occurred to her that with a master like the Beast, they might have been lonely and perhaps even a bit bored. She doubted very much that he had elaborate meals or required much assistance. While at the beginning of the meal she might have thought it silly to feel bad for a talking candelabrum, clock, or teapot, by the end of the meal she had ceased to see any of them as mere objects.

Pushing herself away from the table, Belle thanked everyone and said her good nights. Then she followed Mrs. Potts out of the room. After the warmth and frivolity of the meal, the rest of the castle now seemed colder and darker.

"I don't understand why you're all being so kind to me," Belle said, giving voice to a thought that had been in the back of her mind since she had met Lumiere, Cogsworth, and Mrs. Potts.

Riding atop her serving cart, Mrs. Potts smiled gently. "You deserve nothing less, my love," she said in a sweet motherly tone.

"But you're as trapped here as I am," Belle pointed out. "Don't you ever want to escape?"

Mrs. Potts didn't respond right away. "The master's not as terrible as he appears," she finally said. "Somewhere deep in his soul there's a prince of a fellow, just waiting to be set free."

Belle cocked her head; the words *prince* and *free* sounded like pieces to the puzzle she was trying hard to put together. "Lumiere mentioned something about the West Wing . . ." she went on, hoping to get a bit more information out of the kind teapot.

But Mrs. Potts wasn't falling for it. "Oh, never you mind about that," she said as they reached the bottom of the stairs that led up to Belle's room. "Now off to bed, before the sun starts peeking through the trees. Can I get you anything else, dearie?"

"No, you've already done so much," Belle said sincerely. "Thank you. Good night."

"Nighty-night," Mrs. Potts replied as her serving cart turned and headed back toward the kitchen.

Belle watched, her hand on the railing, until the trolley and Mrs. Potts had disappeared from view. Then she glanced up at the stairs in front of her. She began to climb, her mind whirling. She knew that was her chance to get back to her room and make her escape, yet something was stopping her. She paused on the stairs' landing. If she went to the left, she would get back to her room and, perhaps, freedom. But if she went right . . . She gazed up the set of stairs that must lead to the West Wing.

Her mind made up, Belle took a deep breath. Then she turned right. She still had a little time before sunrise. She would just take a quick peek in the West Wing. After all, what harm could come from a quick look?

CHAPTER IX

BELLE WAS BEGINNING TO THINK SHE had made a very big mistake. While her wing of the castle wasn't exactly bright and colorful, it was a breath of fresh air in comparison with the West Wing. As she walked down the long corridor, her eyes widened. The place *felt* lonely. And it looked downright depressing. The walls were scratched and bare, though it was clear from the empty picture hooks that still hung that hadn't always been the case. The rug beneath her feet was faded and worn, torn in spots by the Beast's long claws. Even the air was heavier somehow.

Belle was on the verge of turning around when she saw light at the end of the hall. A door had been left slightly ajar and through it, Belle could just make out what looked to be a huge suite. Curiosity overtaking her fear, Belle walked forward and slowly pushed open the door.

Instantly, she wished she hadn't. If the hallway had been unnerving, this room was ten times more so. Everywhere she looked she could see evidence of the Beast's temper. Curtains hung in shreds from their rods. Vases that must once have been beautiful lay shattered on the ground. On the huge four-poster bed, a gray coverlet lay, faded and covered in dust, clearly long since used. As her eyes drifted over the room, she saw the reason why. Tucked in a corner was a sort of giant nest made from torn bits of fabric, feathers, and antlers that had been shoved together. Belle felt a rush of foreboding at the sight of such a wild and animalistic area in the castle.

She turned and shouted as she found herself staring at a pair of bright blue eyes. For one long, tense moment she thought someone was staring right back at her—until she realized that the eyes belonged to a boy captured in what was clearly a royal portrait. Her heart thudding, Belle leaned forward. The boy's face had been slashed beyond recognition, that part of the canvas in pieces. But the eyes had been left untouched. Belle leaned still closer. They looked so familiar. . . .

Her breath caught in her throat as Belle realized that they reminded her of the Beast's eyes. Mrs. Potts's words came back to her. *A prince of a fellow*, she had said. This must have been the prince she was referring to. She glanced again at the portrait, looking for clues to the past. There were two other people in the portrait—a handsome king and beautiful queen. And though the woman's image—which included kind eyes full of laughter and love—was still pristine, the king's cold, distant stare had been slashed, as well. Belle wondered what the boy in the portrait must have been like, what *anyone* would have been like, growing up with parents such as those, inside these castle walls.

As Belle dragged her eyes from the portrait and tamped down the odd feeling of melancholy that once again formed in the pit of her stomach, her attention was drawn to the far end of the room. Huge doors had been left open, revealing a large stone balcony on the other side. But it was what was in front of the doors that caught her interest. Amid the chaos and destruction of the room, the table would have stood out just based on the fact it was still upright. But it especially caught her eye because of the glass jar that sat on its surface.

The jar was made of delicate glass, blown so thin it seemed as though it could break with the slightest of touches. Intricate patterns had been etched into the jar's side, looking like frost on a windowpane. And inside, floating as if by magic, was a beautiful red rose. It glowed, the color rivaling that of the most beautiful sunset Belle had ever seen.

As if in a trance, Belle made her way to the table. Slowly, she reached her hand toward the jar. Belle's fingers tingled as she moved them closer to the smooth glass, unable to resist the sudden rush of desire to lift the bell jar and touch the rose's silky petals. Her fingers inched closer . . . closer still . . . and closer . . .

"What are you doing here?" The Beast's voice roared over Belle, shocking her out of her trancelike state. He

appeared from the shadows, his blue eyes blazing, his paws clenched with barely controlled rage. He looked at the glowing rose and the fire in his eyes grew wilder. *"What did you do to it?"*

She quickly backed away from the table. "No—not—nothing," Belle stuttered, her heart thudding in her chest.

The Beast kept coming toward her. "Do you realize what you could have done?" he snarled. "You could have damned us all!" Lashing out, the Beast's claws tore into one of the thin columns that accented the balcony doors. There was a terrible ripping sound and the column began to crumble, pieces shattering and falling close to the glass bell jar holding the rose.

Panic filled the Beast's eyes. Not looking back at Belle, he threw his body over the rose, desperate to protect it. *"Get out!"* he roared over his shoulder.

Belle didn't need to be told twice. Turning, she fled back the way she had come. She ran through the room and out the open door. Then she raced down the long hallway and the even longer stairs. She barely registered the shocked looks of Lumiere and Cogsworth as she passed them on the landing, and when they asked where she was going, she didn't stop to speak to them. "Getting out of here!" she cried over her shoulder and kept running.

Because that was exactly what she was going to do—get out. It was what she *should* have done already. But she had been distracted by Lumiere and his dinner entertainment, and then the castle mystery had lured her in further. But she was done with all that. She was going to get out of this place, with its talking dishware and enchanted candles and clocks, and get back to her father. No matter what.

Unfortunately, the castle didn't want to see Belle leave just yet. Hitting the bottom of the grand staircase, she ran straight toward the front door. To her dismay, the door seemed to see her coming, and before she could reach it, the bolt slid shut. Chapeau, the tall coatrack, slid in front of the door a moment later, blocking Belle's exit.

Belle's pace slowed. What was she going to do now? She didn't know the castle well enough to go running through it blindly trying to find another exit. Then, just as she was about to give up hope, she heard the sound of a dog barking. Turning, she saw Froufrou, the dog turned piano stool, who had run of the castle. He barked wildly as he gave chase and for a brief moment, Belle was worried he was going to pounce on her.

But to her surprise, he ran right past her and scooted through a smaller door that was built into the much larger main door. Belle nearly cried out. Her way out hadn't been blocked. Once again picking up her pace, she shimmied through the smaller door, but not before grabbing her cloak from a befuddled Chapeau. Behind her, Belle heard Mrs. Potts's tea tray rolling across the floor and Lumiere shouting. Still, she kept running.

It didn't take Belle long to find Philippe. The big animal had made himself quite comfortable in one of the stable's roomy stalls. Hearing Belle's footsteps on the cobblestones, he looked up mid-mouthful of hay and cocked his head as if to ask, *What are you doing here?*

Throwing the saddle over his back, Belle didn't answer his questioning look. She pulled him out of the stall instead and quickly mounted. Then she gave his sides a kick. Philippe didn't hesitate. He broke into a canter and headed toward the castle's gate.

Moments later, they were safely through the gate and back in the woods that surrounded the castle.

But it didn't take long for Belle to realize she had traded one terrifying situation for another. As Philippe cantered along, she caught glimpses of shadows out of the corners of her eyes. They gradually grew larger and more clear, and by the time Belle heard the first howl, she already knew that she and Philippe were being followed by a pack of wolves.

Urging Philippe on, Belle tried not to panic. Philippe was a big horse with heavy hooves and he was fast when he needed to be. If they could just get close enough to the village, she was sure the wolves would be frightened by the signs of civilization. As long as they didn't run into any obstacles before then, they should be okay.

And then Philippe ran right out onto a frozen pond.

Beneath his hooves, the ice groaned. Belle leaned over and saw cracks begin to appear. Small at first, they grew larger as the horse slipped and slid across the frozen surface. Shouting encouragement, Belle tried to calm Philippe, who was growing more and more panicked as the ice began to give out beneath him and the wolves closed in from behind. Belle felt the horse's powerful haunches bunch beneath him and she grabbed a fistful of his mane. Then . . . he leapt.

Belle's breath caught in her throat as they hung, suspended in the air for a moment, before Philippe's front hooves landed on the pond's edge. A moment later, his back hooves followed. But the cry of relief Belle wanted to let out caught in her throat as the first of the wolves, seeing a chance, attacked.

One wolf's large jaws snapped as it went after Philippe's back leg. A moment later, another wolf joined in. Philippe kicked out and bucked wildly, trying to defend himself. On his back, Belle clung to his mane desperately. But Philippe was just too strong and powerful. As his hind legs once again flew into the air, she was knocked out of the saddle and went flying into a nearby snowbank.

Getting to her feet, Belle looked around wildly for something she could use to defend herself. Spotting a thick branch, she grabbed it and waved it in the air in front of her.

The wolves, seeing a new and potentially easier target, closed in. Belle's arm shot out and she managed to hit one on the nose. Another came at her and she swung the branch, slamming it into that wolf's side. Despite her efforts, the wolves kept coming. Belle backed up, her heart pounding and fear flooding over her. Hearing a howl from above, she saw the biggest wolf yet standing on a ledge above her, ready to pounce. It stared at her with cold, hungry eyes.

Belle braced, ready to defend herself until the end.

Then she heard a yelp and a thud, and there was a flurry of movement behind her.

Turning, she was shocked to see the Beast. He had leapt into the middle of the pack of wolves. Several of them had backed away and looked to be licking wounds. The largest of the wolves—the alpha—was still on his feet, hackles raised, teeth bared. The Beast's back was to Belle and she could see where the wolves had bitten him. One after another, the smaller of the wolves attacked. Each time, the Beast managed to pick them up and hurl them away. But Belle could tell that the Beast was growing tired. The wounds on his back were bleeding and his head was hanging lower and lower. She wasn't sure how much fight he had left in him.

Then the alpha attacked.

The big gray wolf leapt up onto the Beast's back in one fluid motion. The alpha's mouth opened as he went for the Beast's neck. Roaring, the Beast dropped the two smaller wolves he had been holding in his paws and reached over his shoulder. Just as the alpha's jaws were about to close, the Beast ripped the creature off his back. The alpha's back legs dangled in the air as the Beast, for one long moment, just held him in front of his face, their eyes locked. And then the Beast, with the last of his energy, hurled the alpha away from him. The wolf flew through the air and slammed, with a crack, against a large stone.

Seeing their leader knocked unconscious, the rest of the wolves took off in a panic.

The Beast waited until the wolves' yelps had all but gone before letting out a whimper of pain. His shoulders, which had been tensed and high, slumped. And then he collapsed in the snow. Where his wounds touched the ground, the bright white powder turned red.

Belle stood, unable to move. She was as rooted to the ground as the trees around her. Looking down to where the Beast lay, she knew this was her chance to run. There was no way he could follow her or even try to stop her. Not in his condition. As she watched, he whimpered again and tried to clean one of the wounds on his arm. His blue eyes met hers for just the briefest of moments. But it was long enough for Belle to see the pain and vulnerability in them and for her to make a decision: she wasn't going to leave him there, hurt in the snow. She couldn't. Not after what he had just done for her.

Racing over, she knelt down beside him, pulling off her cloak and laying it over him. "You have to help me," she whispered gently. "You have to stand. . . ." Putting her body under his shoulder, she pushed up, letting the Beast lean on her like a crutch. He roared in pain and grew heavier as the sensation overtook him. Belle shivered. She needed to get the Beast back to the castle—before it was too late.

CHAPTER X

"LISTEN! WOLVES! WE MUST BE close to the haunted castle!"

Sitting in the back of Gaston's carriage, Gaston and LeFou were startled by Maurice's shout. The three men had been making their way through the forest for quite some time. The rest of the crowd had turned back, happy to return to the warmth of the tavern, once Gaston made it clear he was going into the woods. And while the forest wasn't exactly picturesque, it wasn't nearly as menacing as Maurice's wild tavern tale had led Gaston to believe.

"Maurice, enough is enough," Gaston said, turning to look at the older man. The carriage ride had made his wild white hair even more disheveled and his eyes were whipping back and forth as he gazed around the forest desperately. "We have to turn back," Gaston added, not sure Maurice had even heard a word he said.

But apparently he had, because he quickly shook his head. "No! Look!" Maurice pointed up ahead.

Following the old man's finger, Gaston saw a tree on the side of the road. It was withered, its branches bent at odd angles, its trunk smooth with age. Over the course of their journey, Maurice had been telling them all about how he had first found the enchanted castle. He had mentioned something about a tree that looked like a cane and a hidden path. . . . Cocking his head to the side, Gaston narrowed his eyes. It *sort of* looked cane-like, but there was definitely no path behind it.

"That is the tree!" Maurice exclaimed, as if sensing Gaston's doubt. "I'm sure of it. Of course, it was downed by lightning at the time, but now it's been restored to an upright position. By magic, it seems . . ."

Leaning over, LeFou tapped Gaston on the shoulder. "You really want to marry into this family?" he whispered, rolling his eyes.

Gaston knew the smaller man was teasing him,

but LeFou had a point. Enough was enough. He had let Maurice lead them out there with the sole intention of blackmailing him into giving Gaston Belle's hand in marriage. But if they couldn't find Belle, what was the point? "I'm done playing this game of yours," Gaston snapped, stopping the carriage. Jumping down, he put his hands on his hips. "Where is Belle?"

"The Beast took her!" Maurice said again.

Gaston's eyes narrowed. He was trying very hard not to lose his temper, but the old man was making it difficult. "There are no such things as beasts, or talking teacups, or . . . whatever." As he spoke, his voice grew louder and his hands began to clench and unclench at his sides. "But there *are* wolves, frostbite, and starvation."

Scrambling off the carriage, LeFou raced over to his friend's side. "Deep breaths, Gaston," he said. "Deep breaths."

Gaston's jaw clenched, and for a moment, it seemed a very good possibility that he was going to hit something. But then he took a deep breath, like LeFou had suggested. And another. And then one more, for good measure. "So," he started again when he was calmer, "why don't we just turn around and go back to Villeneuve? Belle's probably at home cooking up a lovely dinner. . . ."

"You think I've made all this up?" Maurice asked, seemingly unaware how close Gaston was to breaking. He looked up at the large man in confusion. "If you didn't believe me, why did you offer to help?"

"Because I want to marry your daughter," Gaston said, with no attempt to hide his plan any longer. "Now let's go home."

"I told you! She's not at home, she's with the—"

Rage flooded over Gaston and he erupted. *"If you say 'beast' one more time, I will feed you to the wolves!"* he screamed, all his composure gone. He stalked over to Maurice and raised his fists.

LeFou watched his friend go dark. He knew he had to do something. "Stop!" he cried, frantically trying to think of what to say next. When Gaston got angry, it was hard to pull him out of it. LeFou had really only seen him that way a few times—and it took a while to talk him down. Suddenly, LeFou knew exactly what to do. "Think happy thoughts," he said soothingly. "Go back to the war. Blood, explosions, more blood." As LeFou spoke, the red faded from Gaston's cheeks and his hands began to unclench. His eyes clouded over as he got lost in the memories of his glory days.

By the time LeFou finished speaking, Gaston was back in a good head space. "Please, forgive me," he said. "That's no way to talk to my future father-in-law, now is it?" He smiled at the old man. But the smile didn't reach Gaston's eyes.

That wasn't lost on Maurice. And neither was the fact that Gaston clearly had a dark side. "Captain," he said, backing up a step, "now that I've seen your true face, you'll *never* marry my daughter."

LeFou gulped. *I wouldn't have said that if I were you*, he thought. *Gaston might take it badly and if that happens . . .*

Gaston pulled back and hit Maurice. Hard. The old man sagged to the ground, unconscious.

You might just end up getting hit, LeFou finished his thought. He opened his mouth to try to once again calm his friend down, but it was too late. Gaston had given in to his rage, and there was no pulling him out of it. Not now, at least.

"If Maurice won't give me his blessing," Gaston said as he picked up the unconscious man and carried him over to a tree, "then he is in my way." He pulled a rope out of the carriage and tied Maurice's hands. He gave the knot a tug, checking to make sure it was secure. "Once the wolves are finished with him, Belle will have no one to take care of her but *me*." With an evil laugh, Gaston climbed back into the carriage.

LeFou swayed nervously on his feet as he looked back and forth between Gaston and Maurice. He understood his friend was upset. Gaston *hated* when he didn't get his way. But leaving the old man out there to be eaten by wolves? The punishment seemed a bit severe. "For the sake of exhausting our options," he said nervously, "do we maybe want to consider a plan B?"

Gaston shot him a look. LeFou gulped and quickly

got in the carriage, trying to ignore the pit in his stomach.

It looked like they were sticking to plan A.

Belle had never had a patient who was as beastly as, well, the Beast. Granted, she had only ever tended her father's odd scratch or cut, but at least he had the common courtesy to be polite. Ever since she had gotten the Beast back to the castle, he had been nothing but cranky. And Belle was growing rather tired of it. He hadn't been the one who'd had to walk back through the snowy woods in thin shoes. Nor had *he* been the one who spent that entire journey fearing for his own life. No. The Beast had been unconscious through it all. It had been *Belle* who had anxiously looked over her shoulder at any little sound. It had been *Belle* who'd worried that, with each passing minute, the Beast grew weaker and closer to death.

She hadn't realized just how tense she had been until she and Philippe arrived back at the castle gates and Mrs. Potts appeared at the front door, the staff in tow to help. Then, and only then, had Belle let out a huge breath and allowed herself to start shaking. And once she started, it had taken a long time—and a very hot bath—to stop.

But that was then and this was now. Now she had her hands full trying to treat the Beast, who was proving to be a big baby when it came to pain.

While Belle had recovered, Mrs. Potts had ordered him taken up to his room in the West Wing. He now lay in his old bed, with members of the household staff gathered around to see if they might be of service. A pitcher of hot water and a bowl had been placed beside the bed. Pouring some of the water into the bowl, Belle added a pinch of salt before dipping a clean cloth into the mixture. She rang out the cloth and then, ever so gently, dabbed it on a gash on the Beast's arm.

He roared, as though she had cut him anew. "That hurts!" he snarled, baring his fangs and trying to pull his arm out of reach.

"If you held still, it wouldn't hurt as much," Belle retorted, grabbing his arm and yanking it back.

"If *you* hadn't run away," the Beast said, his jaw clenched, "this wouldn't have happened."

"Well if *you* hadn't frightened me, I wouldn't have run away."

Watching the pair bicker, Mrs. Potts raised an eyebrow. Then she looked over at Lumiere, who hovered nervously by the door. They exchanged knowing glances but remained silent, both curious to see where this new sense of familiarity would lead.

"Well . . ." the Beast went on, determined to get in the last word, "*you* shouldn't have been in the West Wing."

Belle wasn't going to back down. "Well . . . *you* should learn to control your temper."

The Beast's mouth opened, then shut. Then opened again. And shut again. Finally, he let out a small sigh. She had him there.

Smiling, Belle looked back down at the wound she was cleaning. The smile faded. Despite the bickering banter, she was honestly worried about the Beast. The wound was worse than she had initially thought. "Try and get some rest," she said, gently giving it one last dab with the towel. Standing up, she watched as the Beast's eyes slowly closed and his breath grew even. When she was sure he was asleep, and momentarily pain-free, she turned to leave the room. To her surprise, Mrs. Potts and Lumiere were waiting by the door. She had completely forgotten they were there.

"Thank you, miss," Mrs. Potts said, smiling gratefully up at Belle from where she sat perched on the serving tray.

Lumiere bowed. "We are eternally grateful," he added.

Belle nodded, surprised by the deep concern and worry she saw in their eyes. From everything she knew of the Beast, he wasn't a particularly kind master. Yet these two looked nearly as drained as the Beast himself. "Why do you care so much about him?" The question was out of her mouth before she could think to stop herself.

"We've looked after him all his life," Mrs. Potts replied matter-of-factly.

"But he has cursed you somehow," Belle said. She *wanted* to understand why they had such loyalty. It just seemed so . . . strange. When neither the teapot nor the candelabrum responded, she pressed on. "Why? You did nothing."

The Beast's cry from when she'd almost touched the glowing rose echoed in her ears: *You could have damned us all!* The castle was clearly under some sort of spell. And she couldn't imagine any of the castle's *staff* was responsible for their state.

"You're quite right there, dear," Mrs. Potts said. "You see, when the master lost his mother, and his cruel father took that sweet, innocent lad and twisted him up to be just like him . . . we did nothing." As if she had been waiting to tell their story for a long time, the words poured from Mrs. Potts. She painted a sad picture of a young boy who loved his mother with all his heart. Back then, Mrs. Potts told Belle, the castle had been a different place. It had been full of laughter and love, sunshine and innocence.

And then the boy's mother, the *Beast's* mother, Belle

clarified in her head, had grown ill. Belle's eyes grew wide as Mrs. Potts explained that the boy had stayed by his mother's bedside day and night, watching as she withered away. He had begged the doctors to help her but they just shook their heads and offered up false promises.

The poor boy, Belle thought. *I never knew my mother, and I still feel the hole in my heart from where she should be.* She couldn't imagine what it must have been like for the Beast. To have known such love—and lost it.

As if sensing her thoughts, Mrs. Potts went on with her sad tale. After the boy's mother had passed, nothing was ever the same again. The father was a cold, heartless man who tore the sunshine from his son and buried it deep down. As time had passed, all traces of happiness were taken from the castle, replaced with darkness and a sense of heartlessness—even before the curse.

Mrs. Potts's voice trailed off as, on his bed, the Beast moaned in pain. The three watched, their breath held, until he once again settled. As she turned back to Mrs. Potts and Lumiere, Belle's eyes fell on the glass jar and the rose that was slowly fading inside, the crimson petals gathered beneath it.

"What happens when the last petal falls?" she asked, afraid she already knew the answer.

"The master remains a beast forever," Lumiere replied. "And the rest of us become . . ."

"Antiques," Mrs. Potts finished.

"Knickknacks," Lumiere added.

Cogsworth, who had come to check on the patient midway through the conversation, cleared his throat. "Rubbish," he said harshly. "We become rubbish." Belle raised an eyebrow. The clock's voice was more severe than she had ever heard it.

All around her, the other members of the staff who had been helping tend to the Beast joined in, adding to the laundry list of what they would become. Belle listened, her heart growing sad. She knew what it felt like to be trapped. She felt that way living in Villeneuve, where every day was the same, every person like the others. The difference was, she *could* leave if she ever really wanted to get away. Mrs. Potts? Lumiere? Cogsworth? They couldn't. They were stuck inside the castle walls and, she now knew, stuck inside the objects they had become, as well. She turned and looked at the sleeping beast. Like his staff, he was trapped, too. He had been trapped for a long, long time—first by a cruel father and then by this curse.

"I want to help you," Belle said, surprising herself and the others. "There must be some way to lift the curse."

There was a heavy pause as the staff exchanged looks. Then Cogsworth spoke. "Well, there is *one*—"

"It's not for you to worry about, lamb," Mrs. Potts said, stopping Cogsworth. "We've made our bed and we must lie in it." Her statement clear, Mrs. Potts ushered the rest of the staff out of the room.

Belle watched them go. When she was alone with the Beast, she walked over to where he lay. She was surprised to see his eyes were open. He had heard

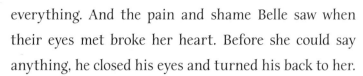

everything. And the pain and shame Belle saw when their eyes met broke her heart. Before she could say anything, he closed his eyes and turned his back to her.

Sighing, Belle retreated and left him to sleep. But as she shut the door, she took one last look at the rose. As she watched, another petal fell. She wished there was something she could do to help the poor souls trapped there. But it all seemed a lost cause, as hopeless as turning back the hands of time.

CHAPTER XI

BELLE DECIDED THAT AS LONG AS SHE was in the castle, she would use her time productively, which for starters meant helping the Beast recover.

Adjusting her dress around her legs, Belle settled into the chair beside the Beast's bed. The Beast's eyes were closed, which gave Belle the chance to assess his wounds. It had been a few days since he'd saved her from the wolves, and with constant care, most of the cuts were beginning to heal. Still, the larger and deeper ones remained bandaged. Those would take longer to heal and were likely to leave scars. Gazing at him, Belle felt a surge of sadness for the creature. He already had so many invisible scars after growing up without a mother to protect him from a cruel father. It seemed unfair that he now had physical ones to match.

Belle sighed. It would do the Beast no good for *her* to sit there feeling sorry for him. Looking around for something she could do to entertain herself while he slept, Belle wasn't surprised to find very little in the way of entertainment. There were no books on the bedside table. The art was all torn and even the furniture was worse for wear. *It looks like I'll just have to make my own entertainment*, Belle thought.

Softly, she recited some of her favorite lines from one of her favorite works, *A Midsummer Night's Dream*. "Love can transpose to form and dignity. Love looks not with the eyes but with the mind."

To her surprise, the Beast's deep voice joined hers and they finished the verse in unison. "And therefore is winged Cupid painted blind."

Belle looked over, eyes wide. The Beast had apparently *not* been sleeping. He was gazing back at her, an amused expression on his hairy face.

"You know Shakespeare?" Belle asked. She knew her voice was filled with disbelief and she blushed. After what Mrs. Potts had told her, she now knew the Beast had once been a human boy. A human *prince*. Still, she couldn't quite wrap her head around the fact that the creature lying on the bed before her seemed to have more class than a great majority of those who lived in her village.

The Beast shrugged. "I had an expensive education," he replied.

There was an awkward pause. "Actually, *Romeo and Juliet* is my favorite play," Belle finally offered.

"Why is that not a surprise?" the Beast replied, a hint of a smile in his eyes.

"Sorry?" Belle said, feigning offense.

"All that heartache and pining and—" The Beast shuddered dramatically. "There are so many better things to read."

"Like *what*?" Belle said, raising an eyebrow. She crossed her arms, the challenge thrown down.

The Beast smiled. Then he began to push himself up.

"Oh, no you don't!" Belle said, reaching out to stop him.

But even wounded, the Beast was far stronger than

Belle. He brushed her off and got out of the bed. Then, without a word, he slowly made his way out of the room. Belle had no choice but to follow.

By the time they made it down the West Wing's long hallway, turned several corners, and climbed one smaller staircase, Belle was nearly bubbling over with curiosity. The Beast had not said a word or given a hint as to where they were going. He just walked slowly, pausing every now and then to catch his breath.

Finally, they came to a stop in front of a pair of grand doors, which soared at least two stories high and were intricately carved with reliefs depicting various scenes. Standing next to the Beast, Belle tried to make out some of the larger ones, but before she could, the Beast pushed open the doors. "There are a couple of things in here you can start with," he said.

Belle gasped.

In front of her was the most beautiful thing she had ever seen. It was a library. But this was not just any library. This had to be the biggest, grandest library in all of France. The ceiling soared above her, shelves full of books going all the way to the very top. A massive fireplace dominated one wall, and even on the mantel, books were displayed. On another wall, a large window let in plenty of light to read by, but even still, candles were lit throughout the chamber. Despite its immense size, the room was comfortable, cozy. Belle looked around at the multitude of deep cushioned chairs and imagined how peaceful it would be to curl up in one with a book in hand.

"Are you all right?" the Beast asked, his voice laced with genuine concern.

Belle imagined she looked like a fish gaping in water for how shocked and awestruck she felt. She turned and smiled up at him. "It's wonderful," she said, knowing that was not grand enough a response to a room such as this.

"Why, yes, I suppose it is," the Beast said thoughtfully, as though noticing this for the first time. "Well then it is yours. You can be master here." He bowed and turned to leave.

Belle's voice stopped him. Her neck was craned back

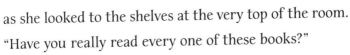

as she looked to the shelves at the very top of the room. "Have you really read every one of these books?"

"Not all of them," the Beast replied. "Some are in Greek."

Belle's mouth dropped open. "Was that a joke?" she said, beginning to smile. "Are you making jokes now?"

The Beast tried not to smile as he replied, "Maybe . . ."

Without another word, the Beast turned and left the room. Belle remained where she was, shaking her head as he made his exit. What had just happened?

As the days passed, Belle found more and more reason to ask herself that same question. Instead of what *had* happened, however, it quickly became what *was* happening? Because there was no denying it—something had changed between Belle and the Beast. She wasn't sure if it had started when he rescued her in the woods or when she had turned around and rescued *him.* Or perhaps it had been the afternoon he shared the library with her and she first saw the softer side of him. It might have even started somewhere in between all that—when Mrs. Potts had told her the story of the Beast's youth. *When it had happened didn't matter.* What mattered, what Belle could not deny, was the simple truth that there was a spark of something between them that hadn't been there before. Something that made the days at the castle feel less like a prison sentence and more—well, more like fun.

And the Beast had become less like her captor and more of a friend.

Belle no longer snuck down to the kitchen to get her meals. Instead, she and the Beast shared the dining room table—he at one end, she at the other. Sometimes they would each bring a book and read at the table in companionable silence. At other meals, they would talk about the books, sharing their favorite parts or what they would have changed. So caught up in their mutual love of reading was she that Belle stopped noticing when the Beast slurped his soup straight from the bowl and ignored the silverware entirely. Sometimes she even went so far as to sip the soup the same way, to make the Beast feel more comfortable.

Meals and books were not the only things they shared. When the weather permitted, Belle would join the Beast outside as he showed her around the grounds, or they would walk Philippe. And even when the weather wasn't perfect, they found ways to enjoy themselves outside the castle walls. Snowy days led to snowball fights; sunny days led to picnics.

Belle even encouraged the Beast to help her and the castle staff clean up the castle—the two of them scrubbing the floors until the old gleaming marble shone through, wiping the years of grime off the windows until they saw sparkling sunlight. They transformed the West Wing, removing the shattered columns and debris and replacing the torn bits of fabric with cozy blankets to make a proper bed for the Beast.

With each moment and adventure they shared, Belle grew more and more comfortable around the Beast.

She no longer shuddered if he accidently brushed her with his paw. Nor did her smile fade when his flashed, revealing sharp fangs.

In fact, Belle realized with a start at lunch one afternoon, she didn't even really see those parts of him anymore. She saw the kindness in his eyes when he looked at her. She heard the intelligence in his voice when they debated literature. And she saw the pride he had in his home when he looked around.

I'm seeing the man inside the Beast, she wrote one afternoon in a diary she'd started keeping. If her current experiences didn't warrant a journal, she didn't know what did. *I'm seeing what Mrs. Potts and Lumiere and Cogsworth and all the others have seen all along. It just took me some time. . . .* Closing the pages, Belle stood up and went to the window of her elegant room. Outside, the last of the day's light was fading. A nearly full moon was beginning to peek over the horizon, illuminating the snowy gardens below in a pale, ethereal light. Looking out, Belle was struck once again by the beauty of the castle. Since her friendship with the Beast had grown stronger, and they had made the effort to return the estate to its former glory, the whole castle had become brighter and cheerier right before her very eyes. She saw the beauty in the lines of the stone that made up the castle walls and appreciated the towering turrets. It was not the quaint and picturesque architecture of Villeneuve but it was enchanting nonetheless.

Spotting the Beast making his way toward the colonnade, book in hand, Belle turned and grabbed her own book from the bedside table. Making her way downstairs and outside, she went to join him.

"What are you reading?" she asked when she, too, had entered the colonnade.

The Beast looked up, startled to see her. He dropped the book to his side. "Nothing," he said, trying to hide it from Belle.

It was too late. Belle had already seen the title. "Guinevere and Lancelot," she observed.

The Beast shrugged. "King Arthur and the round table," he clarified. "Swords, fighting . . ." His attempt to focus on the more action-packed parts of the book was not lost on Belle.

"Still . . . it's a romance," she pointed out, trying not to smile as the Beast shrugged and looked sheepish.

"Felt like a change," he finally said.

For a moment, the pair just stood there in somewhat awkward silence. Despite all the time they had been spending together, this felt different to Belle. Maybe it was the moonlight. Maybe it was the Beast's admission of change. Maybe it was just a shift in the air. Whatever the reason, Belle felt a sudden compulsion to say something she had not said before. "I never thanked you for saving my life," she finally said softly.

"I never thanked you for not leaving me to die," he responded without hesitation, as though he, too, had been wanting to say the words for a long while but had never found the right time.

The air crackled between them as they stood, eyes locked, their words lingering in the air. Just when Belle was sure it couldn't get any more tense, they heard shouts followed by laughter coming from inside the castle. The servants, it seemed, were having a nice fete. The noise broke the tension and both Belle and the Beast smiled in relief.

"Well . . . they know how to have a good time," Belle said.

The Beast nodded. "Sometimes, when I take my dinner, I listen to their laughter and pretend I am eating with them."

"You should!" Belle said, impressed he would admit such a thing. "They'd love that."

"No, I've tried," he replied, the moment of levity gone as quickly as it had come. "When I enter a room, laughter dies."

Belle's mouth opened and shut. That was *exactly* how she felt whenever she went into town. She said as much to the Beast. Then she added, "The villagers say that I'm a funny girl, but I don't think they mean it as a compliment." To her surprise, she felt tears prick at the backs of her eyes. She had never admitted to anyone that it hurt her feelings—not even her father.

"I'm sorry," the Beast said, his tone genuine. "Your village sounds terrible."

"Almost as lonely as your castle," Belle said.

Once again the Beast nodded, not offended by her statement. Over the past few days, Belle's presence—and the life she breathed into the castle—had shown him just how lonely a place the castle had been. "It wasn't always like this," he said. He paused as an idea came to him, then gave her a smile. "What do you say we run away?"

Belle cocked her head, surprised by the suggestion. That was the *last* thing she had expected to hear come out of the Beast's mouth. Intrigued, she nodded and followed as he led her out of the colonnade and back into the castle. And despite the many questions she had forming in the back of her mind, she remained quiet as he led her down now familiar hallways and up a flight of stairs to the library.

With purpose, the Beast walked over to a simple desk that was tucked against one of the library's walls.

Pulling a key out of his pocket, he unlocked one of the cabinets.

Belle peered over his shoulder. Resting on a pillow made of rich velvet was the most beautiful book Belle had ever seen. The leather cover was lined with gold leaf and glimmered despite the thick layer of dust on top. It seemed magical to Belle and she longed to reach out and touch it.

"The Enchantress gave me this," the Beast said, turning and seeing Belle's wide eyes. "Another of her many curses." He slowly opened it, the spine cracking with lack of use. There was no writing, no title page or dedication. Instead, the first page opened to reveal an antique world atlas. Unlike ordinary atlases, this one did not show countries or capitals. It just showed land and sea. Belle looked up at the Beast, a questioning look in her eye. "A book that truly allows you to escape," he answered.

Stepping forward, Belle's eyes grew still wider as she saw the art come to life. Waves lapped against

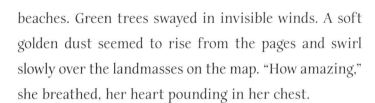

beaches. Green trees swayed in invisible winds. A soft golden dust seemed to rise from the pages and swirl slowly over the landmasses on the map. "How amazing," she breathed, her heart pounding in her chest.

The Beast did not seem as impressed. "It was the Enchantress's cruelest trick of all," he said softly. "The outside world has no place for a monster like me. But it can for you." Slowly, he reached out and took Belle's hand in his. Then he gently moved it to the book. "Think of the place you've most wanted to see. First see it in your mind's eye. Now feel it in your heart."

Belle closed her eyes. She didn't need to think of a place she wanted to see. She knew it instinctively. Reaching out her fingers, Belle placed them on the page. Instantly, the room around them began to spin and the library walls seemed to fade away.

When Belle opened her eyes, she was no longer looking at the floor-to-ceiling bookshelves. The snow-covered peaceful gardens had vanished and the stars had faded. They were standing in a small dusty apartment with a view of glittering lights shining from a city skyline.

The Beast gazed out the window and saw the wooden blade of a windmill move past. "Where did you take us?"

"Paris," Belle said, her whisper barely audible over the sound of the Montmartre windmill's blades rushing by.

"Oh, I love Paris," the Beast exclaimed. "What would you like to see first? Notre Dame? The Champs-Élysées? Too touristy?"

But Belle was absorbed in her own thoughts, looking around the little dim room they were standing in. She had thought about this particular apartment for so many years, had pictured it in her mind's eye. But she had never dared dream she would see it for real. Her eyes brimmed with tears. "It's so much smaller than I imagined," she said after a moment, blinking back the tears.

They had been transported to the dusty attic where Belle had lived with her father and mother so many years before. It looked abandoned, a small crib and broken easel the only reminders that the place had once been a home. As Belle walked forward, the sadness she had felt earlier returned with a vengeance. For some reason, she had imagined that the enchanted book would reveal her childhood home as it had been, not as it was now. But what she was looking at was clearly an empty shell of a place. No one had lived there for years—not since Maurice had moved himself and Belle to the country.

Beside her, the Beast kept silent, letting her have the moment and the memories. But as she picked up a rattle that had been caught in the corner of the crib, he finally spoke. "What happened to your mother?" he asked softly.

"That's the only story Papa could never bring himself to tell," Belle said, clutching the rattle in her hand. The wood was old, but the detail was still exquisite. It was a perfectly carved rose. "And I knew well enough not to ask."

As she spoke, the Beast's eyes traveled to the corner

of the room. He moved to pick up a black mask that resembled a bird's beak, his expression pained. That mask meant only one thing: it was what doctors used to prevent catching their patients' dreadful disease. Belle followed his gaze, and as she saw the mask, tears brimmed anew in her eyes. The plague. That was what had taken her mother. That was what had sent her father fleeing for the safety of the country.

All these years, she had resented him for keeping her trapped in Villeneuve. But now she knew what he must have endured. She could picture her mother insisting he take Belle away, insisting they leave her there before they, too, were infected. She could not imagine how it must have felt to watch his beloved slowly die and not be able to save her. Belle's knuckles turned white as her grip on the rose-shaped rattle tightened.

"I am sorry I ever called your father a thief," the Beast said.

Lost in her thoughts, Belle was surprised by the Beast's deep voice. She turned her face up to him. He was staring down at her, concern etched in his features.

Wiping the tears from her eyes, Belle took one last look around the room. She had seen enough. She put the rattle in the pocket of her apron, not wanting to part with it.

Reaching out, she took the Beast's hand. "Let's go home," she said. "To the castle."

The Beast nodded, and together, they placed their hands once more on the pages of the enchanted book, closed their eyes . . . and pictured home.

CHAPTER XII

GASTON WAS GROWING RESTLESS. HE had spent the past few weeks doing what he normally did—hunting, participating in eating contests, taking one of the local girls out for dinner. But he was wondering when Belle would finally return.

Maurice was no doubt long gone. He wasn't going to return to bother Gaston, and when Belle came back from wherever it was she had run off to, the path to their marriage would be clear. Yes, it was all going to work out just fine, Gaston thought as he made his way toward the tavern for his evening dose of adoration and grog. He just needed his future wife to hurry home.

And he needed LeFou to stop talking.

Gaston's constant companion was, once again, babbling on about Maurice—which was making it rather difficult for Gaston to completely put the moment in his past. "Wow, this is some storm," the smaller man was saying. "At least we're not tied to a tree in the middle of nowhere, right? You know, it's not too late. We could just go get him. . . ."

Gaston didn't respond.

LeFou pressed on. "It's just, every time I close my eyes, I picture Maurice stranded out there. And then when I open them, he's . . ."

His voice trailed off as Gaston swung open the doors to the tavern, revealing Maurice.

"Oh, that's funny, I was going to say 'dead,'" LeFou finished, his voice squeaking.

Maurice was surrounded by the usual tavern goers, including Jean the potter and Pere Robert. Other than a red nose, he seemed no worse for the wear, and it was clear from the daggers the villagers were shooting at Gaston that he had felt well enough after his ordeal to tell them all about what had happened.

"Gaston," Jean said, his voice serious, "did you try to kill Maurice?"

Gaston knew he had only a few options. He could fight, which was his usual answer. He could run, but that option was weak and made his skin crawl. So after a quick glance around the room, he decided to go with another option: deny, deny, deny. Plastering a warm smile on his face, he walked quickly to Maurice, who had his arms crossed. "Oh, Maurice," he began. "Thank heavens. I've spent the last five days trying to find you. Why did you run off into the forest in your condition?"

As his words bounced around the room, the villagers who had gathered shuffled, unsure of who to believe.

"What?" Maurice said in disbelief. Then he shook his head. "No! You tried to kill me! You left me for the wolves!"

Gaston put a hand to his chest as though Maurice's words had hurt him. "Wolves? What are you talking about?" he asked. He looked at the villagers and rolled his eyes as if to say, *Are we really going back down this road again? Are you really going to believe him over me?* He tried not to smile smugly when the majority of them returned his eye roll.

"The wolves near the Beast's castle," Maurice answered, his voice rising and adding to his manic appearance.

"That's right," Gaston said condescendingly. "There's a beast with a castle that somehow none of us have ever seen?"

Maurice hesitated. Looking around the room, he saw that everyone was waiting for his answer. "Well . . . yes," he finally said.

Gaston had Maurice—and everyone else—just where he wanted him. Like when he cornered his prey on the hunt, he had Maurice on the defensive, as if Maurice knew his time was running out. Slowly, Gaston shook his head. "It's one thing to rave about your delusions," he said. "It's another to accuse me of murder."

To his surprise, it was Pere Robert, not Maurice, who spoke up. The priest stepped in front of Maurice defensively. Then he looked at the gathered crowd. "Listen to me, all of you," he pleaded. "This is Maurice, our neighbor. Our friend. He is a good man."

Gaston tried not to smile. He could not have set the

situation up for the final blow better if he had tried. "Are you suggesting that I am not?" he said, sounding hurt. "Did I not save this village from the savagery of the Portuguese marauders? Am I not the only reason you people are gathered here this evening and not buried up on the hillside?"

His words, like an arrow shot from his bow, struck home. The villagers mumbled to each other, their growing doubt in Maurice clear.

"Maurice," Jean the potter said, turning to look at the old man, "do you have any proof of what you're saying?"

"Ask Agathe!" he replied, frantically trying to keep the room with him. "She rescued me!" Turning, he pointed to the far dark corner of the tavern where the old beggar woman had been watching everything silently. Feeling everyone's eyes on her, Agathe cowered and pulled her tattered hood tighter around her face.

Gaston raised an eyebrow. "You'd hang your accusation on the testimony of a filthy beggar woman?" he said.

Realizing that might not have been the best of moves, Maurice looked around. He needed to change tactics. Spotting Gaston's ever-present companion, Maurice let out a cry. "Monsieur LeFou! He was there. He saw it all!"

"Me?" LeFou said, gulping as the attention turned to him.

"You're right. Don't take my word for it," Gaston said, once again thrilled by how the whole scene was playing out in his favor. He walked over and put his arm around his friend. "LeFou, my dearest companion, did you and I, *Le Duo*"—he used the nickname, his voice oozing false sincerity—"find any beasts or haunted castles on our search?"

LeFou's head swung back and forth. On his shoulder, Gaston's grip tightened. It was clear what answer *he* wanted to hear. But looking at Maurice, LeFou remembered how bad he had felt as they drove away, leaving him in the cold and dark. Gaston's grip tightened further. "It's a complicated question on a number of accounts, but . . . no?" he finally answered.

"And did I, your oldest friend and most loyal compatriot," Gaston continued, laying it on thick, "try to kill the father of the only woman I've ever loved?"

"Well . . ." LeFou hedged. " 'Kill' is such a strong word. No. No, you didn't."

That was all the crowd needed to hear. Instantly, the tide of good feeling shifted from Maurice to Gaston. As the old man's face fell, a smirk tugged at the corner of Gaston's mouth. He had won. "Maurice, it pains me to say this," he said insincerely, "but you've become a danger to yourself and others. You need help, sir. A place to heal your troubled mind." He walked over and put a large hand on Maurice's shoulder. Then he squeezed, hard. "Everything's going to be fine." But while his words were nice, his tone was as cold as ice.

Maurice gulped. He knew, without a doubt, that nothing was going to be fine. Nothing at all.

Inside the castle, the Beast was having similar thoughts. Time was running out and he was not even remotely sure that things would be all right. And clearly he wasn't the only one. While he had hoped to get ready for that evening alone, an audience had gathered—an audience with an opinion.

"This is it, master," Mrs. Potts said as she entered the West Wing. The Beast was in the large bathroom, immersed in a huge tub of soapy hot water. "Now or never."

"The clock is ticking," Cogsworth added.

"The rose has only four petals left," Lumiere added. "Which means tonight . . . you *must* tell her how you feel."

The Beast sighed. He knew that his staff was just trying to help. Nothing they were saying was a surprise. He *knew* time was running out. He *knew* that night was important. He *knew* Belle was his one chance—the castle's one chance. Hearing it out loud did nothing to ease his growing anxiety. And he did not care to admit how especially nervous he was about the upcoming evening. He had made an offhanded comment to Belle about how beautiful the ballroom looked after all her hard

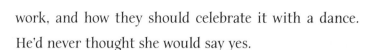

work, and how they should celebrate it with a dance. He'd never thought she would say yes.

He signaled the others to give him a moment of privacy and finished his bath. A curtain had been drawn in front of the tub. He stood and shook himself dry. Finally, he spoke. "She will never love me," he said.

"Do not be discouraged," Lumiere said to the shadow of the Beast behind the curtain. "She is the one."

"There is no *one*," the Beast retorted. He pulled back the curtain and stepped into the light provided by Lumiere's candles. "Look at me. She deserves so much more than a beast."

To Lumiere's credit, he didn't cringe on seeing the Beast, who, at that particular moment, was looking rather, well, silly. His hair was sticking out in every direction from his shaking himself dry, and the towel he had wrapped around his waist only made his large shoulders seem wider and hairier. Lumiere cleared his throat and pressed on. "You care for her, don't you?"

The Beast nodded. He did care for Belle, more than

he ever would have thought possible. The past few days and their trip to Paris had only solidified those feelings. But he was no fool. While he might have come to care for her, and she might have learned to be around him without cringing, that did not mean she loved him in return. He was a beast, after all. No matter how many baths he took, no matter the clothes he wore or if he managed to eat his soup with a spoon, that wasn't going to change—unless she *did* somehow love him as he was. But that was unlikely.

Lumiere saw the doubt and fear in his master's eyes but forged ahead, propelled by his nod. "Well then, woo her with beautiful music and romantic candlelight. . . ."

"Yes," Plumette added, "and when the moment's just right . . ."

The Beast cocked his head. "How will I know?"

Cogsworth, who until that point had been purposely keeping himself out of the conversation, cleared his throat. "In my experience," he said, "you will feel slightly nauseous."

Lumiere shot him a look, silencing the clock. "Don't worry, master," he said, turning back to the Beast. "You'll do fine. The problem has been that until now, the girl could not see the real you."

"No," Mrs. Potts said, disagreeing. "The problem was . . . she *could*."

Instantly, the room grew silent. Tension filled the air as the staff turned and looked at the teapot. Some, like Lumiere, hoped to see a glint of humor in her eye. Others, like Cogsworth, were unsurprised by her sudden announcement. Either way, everyone's attention finally turned to the Beast, whom they watched, with eyes wide, as Mrs. Potts went on.

"For years," she said, "we have hoped against hope that this curse would make you a better man. But you have remained angry and selfish and cruel, and we are all running out of time. And there is one more thing your servants have been too afraid to tell you."

"What?" the Beast asked. He was surprised to discover that he feared her answer. Was she going to tell him exactly how hated he was? Was she going to tell him how miserable they had been and for how long? Was it possible she was going to find a way to make him feel even worse than he already did?

"We love you," Mrs. Potts said.

The Beast nearly staggered back with the weight of her words. Of all the things he had imagined she might say . . .

Mrs. Potts went on. "Until now, we have loved you in spite of how you were. But since that girl arrived, we love you *because* of it." Around her, the servants nodded in agreement. "So stop being a coward and tell Belle how you feel. And if you don't, I promise you'll be drinking cold tea for the rest of your life."

"In the dark," Lumiere added.

"Covered in dust," Plumette chimed in.

In silence, the staff looked up at the Beast and waited for his response.

And then the Beast smiled. Slowly at first, it spread across his face until it took over. And it wasn't the scary smile he had first flashed at Belle. It was a warm smile. It was a genuine smile. It was the smile of a beast who no longer felt alone. It was the smile of a *man* who finally felt hope.

As Belle stood in her room letting Garderobe primp and pamper her, she was struck again by a case of nerves. Ever since she'd agreed to celebrate the restoration of the ballroom with a dance, butterflies had been firmly lodged in her belly. Now, as the moment to go downstairs grew closer, the feeling grew stronger.

Ever since they had returned from Paris, Belle had felt another serious shift in her relationship with the Beast. He had seen her at her most vulnerable and he had been a source of strength for her. Their conversations now went far beyond books. Their walks in the gardens were longer, neither wanting them to end. Belle found herself anticipating dinner, no longer just for the scrumptious food but for the company. If she'd had a friend to talk to, she probably would have admitted that her feelings for the Beast, as unlikely as it seemed, had become deeper than she had ever thought possible.

And now she was about to go spend an evening with

him, dancing in the ballroom. She sighed. How had she gotten here?

Garderobe gave Belle's dress one last adjustment and then turned her around so she was facing the full-length mirror.

Belle gasped. After her first day in the castle, she had been slightly hesitant to let the wardrobe dress her. They had talked about Belle's preference for clothes without frills, for outfits that had practical elements, like hemlines that didn't drag on the floor and pockets—much to Garderobe's chagrin.

But slowly, Garderobe had begun to create ensembles that fit Belle to a tee. And that night, she had outdone herself. Belle didn't even recognize the girl staring back at her with wide brown eyes. Her hair had been pulled back halfway, accenting her cheeks, which had been ever so lightly dusted with blush. And the dress. The dress was something out of Belle's wildest fantasies. It floated around her like a golden halo. With every movement she made, it shone, catching the light and casting it back into the room. Garderobe stretched out one of her drawers, and suddenly, a layer of gold dust magically fell from the ceiling, coating the dress and making it, if possible, still more beautiful. Plus, it was easy to move in, light as a feather.

Pleased with her work, Garderobe pushed Belle out the door.

Belle stood still for a long moment. Her heart pounded. *It is just a night*, she thought. *Stop dilly-dallying and get down those stairs.*

Taking a deep breath, Belle began the long walk down the hall toward the staircase. Reaching the top, she looked across to the top of the West Wing's stairs. To her surprise, the Beast was standing there—clad in his best formal wear, looking as nervous as she felt. Their eyes met. They walked toward each other, meeting on the center landing. Then he bowed his head and extended his arm, inviting her, without words, to join him. She didn't hesitate to take it.

Together, they descended the staircase. With each step, Belle's anxiety faded. It felt normal to be walking with the Beast. And when he started to lead her into the dining room, it was *her* decision to turn to the ball-room instead.

She sensed his hesitation as she led him to the mid-dle of the dance floor. But as quickly as that hesitation had appeared, it disappeared as music magically began to play. The room had been scrubbed clean and lit with hundreds of candles so that everything glowed like the golden dress Belle wore. The stage was set.

And then they began to dance. They waltzed in perfect time, Belle's feet following the Beast's auto-matically. They moved in a series of steps and delicate spins, each partner in tune with the other. It was as though they had been dancing together for years, not minutes, and once again, Belle was struck by how com-fortable she felt around the Beast. As Cadenza reached a crescendo in the music, the Beast lifted Belle so she floated at his side, and then swept her into a thrilling dip. When the music finally came to an end and the ballroom fell into silence, Belle felt a strange tug of sadness that it was over.

As if sensing this, the Beast did not release her hand. Instead, he led her out to the large terrace that circled the ballroom. A companionable silence fell over the pair as they both stared up at the starry sky. The air was crisp, as it always was around the enchanted castle, but not uncomfortable. Belle felt as though the Beast's arms were still wrapped around her, the warmth from the ballroom somehow finding its way outside.

"I haven't danced in years," the Beast said, breaking the silence. "I'd almost forgotten the feeling." He dragged his eyes from the stars and looked down at Belle. His gaze was full of warmth—and something else. He shifted nervously on his feet as though not sure whether to go on. Belle waited, trying to encourage him silently. Then he spoke again. "It's foolish, I suppose, for a creature like me to hope that one day he might earn your affection."

Belle hesitated. It wasn't foolish. At least, moments earlier it hadn't seemed foolish. "I don't know . . ." she said softly.

Hope flared in the Beast's eyes. "Really?" he asked. "You think you could be happy here?"

"Can anybody be happy if they aren't free?" Belle asked softly.

The Beast blinked guiltily, knowing she was right.

An image of Maurice flashed through Belle's mind. "My father taught me to dance. Our house was always filled with music."

"You must miss him," the Beast said, the tone of her voice not lost on him.

Belle nodded. "Very much."

Seeing the tears rise in Belle's eyes, the Beast felt his heart tighten. He hated to see her in pain, especially when he knew there was a way he could ease it. "Come with me," he said, taking her hand.

Silently, he led her off the terrace and back through the ballroom. He didn't answer when she asked where they were going and didn't explain when he brought her into his room and lifted a small hand mirror up to her. All he said was "Show me Maurice." Then he handed the mirror to Belle and waited.

The face of the mirror swirled magically, and within moments, Belle's reflection had been replaced by an image of Maurice. With growing horror, she watched her father being dragged through the village square. Terror was etched on his face and he was calling out to someone to help him.

"Papa!" she cried. "What are they doing to him?"

The Beast had hoped to make Belle happy by showing her Maurice. Her reaction was not what he had anticipated. He peered over her shoulder, and his eyes grew wide as he, too, saw what was happening to the old man. Pain for Belle, for what was happening to her father, overcame him. Then, as Belle continued to watch her father through the mirror, the Beast's gaze shifted to the rose jar.

Another petal dropped.

Mrs. Potts's words echoed in his head. The feeling of Belle's hand in his burned through him. He pictured his staff, their hopeful faces as he had finally gotten dressed for the evening. Then he looked back at Belle and saw the sorrow in her eyes. He knew this was a moment of choice. But he also knew there was no choice to be made. He had to start righting the wrongdoings that he *could* right.

"You must go to him," he said, trying to keep his own pain from his voice.

Belle looked up. "What did you say?" she asked, shocked.

"You are no longer a prisoner here," he went on. "No time to waste."

Tears of gratitude and appreciation replaced her tears of sadness as Belle looked up at the Beast. There was so much she wanted to say. So much she *needed* to say. But she didn't know where to begin. She started to return the mirror, but he shook his head.

"Keep it with you," he said, "so you will have a way to look back on me."

"Thank you," Belle said in a whisper. *Thank you for everything,* she added silently.

And then, before she could change her mind, Belle turned and ran.

CHAPTER XIII

THE BEAST DIDN'T GO BACK DOWN-stairs. He couldn't bear the thought of seeing the expectant, hopeful faces of his staff. Instead, he walked out onto the West Wing balcony, not daring to glance at the bell jar to see how many petals were left on the enchanted rose. From there, he watched Belle race off on Philippe, heard the clanging of the castle gate as it shut behind her, listened until the sound of the horse's hooves faded into silence as it galloped through the woods. And still he did not move. Not even as the clear sky clouded over and the air grew uncomfortably chilly. He just stood there, the increasing wind whipping at his coat, his blue eyes troubled.

His last chance was gone—for good. While they might have just shared a magical evening, he knew somehow that Belle would never return.

After a while, he returned to his room, unclasping his beautiful coat and letting it fall to the ground. Behind him, he heard the unmistakable sound of Cogsworth's waddle.

"Well, master," the majordomo said, his voice chipper, "I may have had my doubts, but everything is moving like clockwork." He smiled at his own wordplay. "True love really does win the day!"

"I let her go," the Beast said, his tone flat. What good was delaying the inevitable? It was a large castle, true, but news spread fast. It would be better just to get it out in the open and deal with the fallout.

Cogsworth's mouth dropped open. "You . . . *what?*"

As if on cue, Lumiere and Plumette entered the room. Mrs. Potts followed on her trolley. From the looks on their faces, the Beast could tell they had heard everything.

"Master . . ." Lumiere said, the flames on his candles growing dim. "How could you do that?"

"I had to," the Beast replied simply.

"But why?" Lumiere and Cogsworth asked in unison.

They were both looking at the Beast with confusion. His behavior was so odd. It was as though the Beast had suddenly become a different person.

"Because he loves her," Mrs. Potts answered for the Beast.

Everyone turned to the teapot. Her voice was soft, her eyes sad as she looked at the Beast. His shoulders slumped, but he did not deny what Mrs. Potts had said. She was right. He did love Belle.

"Then why are we not human?" Lumiere asked, still confused.

Cogsworth, unfortunately, was no longer confused. Now he was mad. "Because *she* doesn't love *him!*" he snapped. "And now it's too late!"

"But she might still come back . . . ?" Plumette suggested hopefully.

The Beast shook his head. "No. I've set her free." He turned his back to the staff. "I'm sorry I couldn't do the same for all of you," he said, meaning it with every fiber of his being.

Then, stepping out onto his balcony, he looked at

the empty stable. Belle's leading Philippe out of the stable had been the hardest thing the Beast had ever had to witness. The pain he had felt in those first few years after the Enchantress had cursed him paled in comparison to the pain he had felt as Belle urged Philippe away. He had let his heart, which had been closed for so long, open, and the result? A deeper wound than he could bear. Because he knew the memory of Belle, like the curse, would now be with him forever.

He left the balcony and began to climb the castle's highest turret. The wind blew against him, threatening to whip him right off the stones, but still he climbed. The menacing gusts were a welcome distraction. But even that wasn't enough to keep images of Belle from flitting across his mind. Reaching the top of the turret, he peered through the woods, hoping for one last glimpse of her. But all he saw were trees. With a groan, he collapsed to the ground. There was no denying it any longer: she was gone for good. All he had left of her, all he would ever have of her, were memories that would fade over time, leaving him alone—and a beast—forever.

Belle urged Philippe on, her heels digging into his sides. She knew the horse was fading, but she needed to get back to Villeneuve. Her father was in danger.

At first, the woods were strange to her and all she could do was hope Philippe remembered where he was going. But soon she began to recognize familiar land-marks. A patch of blueberries here, a small pond there. As the moon rose higher in the sky, she finally burst out of the woods and into the clearing at the edge of the village. She made sure her most prized possessions—the magic mirror and a small satin pouch she'd taken from the castle—were still safely in her lap.

Then, hearing a commotion near the square, Belle steered Philippe in that direction. To her surprise, a crowd had gathered around a horse-drawn wagon, which looked like a small metal prison with its steel frame and tiny barred window. She spotted Gaston and LeFou standing nearby. Gaston looked smug, as always, while LeFou looked uncomfortable. She continued to scan the scene, and then her breath caught in her throat.

Maurice was slumped inside the wagon's cage.

As Belle watched, Pere Robert ran up to the man locking Maurice inside—Monsieur D'Arque, the head of the town asylum. "This man is hurt!" Pere Robert said. "Please! He needs a hospital, not an asylum!"

Ignoring him, D'Arque finished his task and headed up to the driver's perch. Gaston walked over and leaned against the wagon, seeming to whisper something to Maurice.

Belle had seen enough. That wagon wasn't going anywhere. Kicking Philippe forward, she made her way into the middle of the crowd. "Stop!" she cried.

Her voice cut through the crowd, silencing everyone instantly. The people turned in her direction, eyes wide. Her ball gown flowed around her, the gold glitter catching the moonlight and making the dress sparkle magically. She could hear the whispers of the villagers beginning like a slow wave. Some wondered where she had come from. Others wondered if it was really her. Others muttered "that dress" with envy and awe.

Ignoring them, Belle dismounted. She kept her head high, her eyes seeking support in the crowd of villagers. She didn't find much. Most of the villagers were eyeing her with open distrust now that their initial shock had faded. Still, there were a few friendly faces. Pere Robert was standing close by, his expression bewildered and a bit defeated. And Jean the potter was there, too, though he looked puzzled and helpless, as usual.

Pushing down the slew of unkind words she wanted to hurl at the villagers, Belle stepped in front of the wagon. "Stop this right now!" she ordered, causing the horses to startle. She ran to the back of the wagon and peered through the locked door. Her father lay on the floor, clutching his side in pain. "Open this door! He's hurt!"

Monsieur D'Arque climbed down from his perch. As he walked toward her, Belle couldn't help cringing. There was something dark and cruel in his eyes, and his pale skin reminded her of the monsters in some of her stories. "I'm afraid we can't do that, miss," he said. "But we'll take good care of him." While his words were meant to sound reassuring, they came across as a threat.

"My father's not crazy!" Belle protested. She turned and looked around the crowd, hoping for help. No one stepped forward. Finally, she turned to the one man she thought might advocate for her. "Gaston . . . tell him!" she pleaded.

Gaston stepped out of the shadows where he had been waiting quietly. He had been worried that Belle had witnessed his part in Maurice's incarceration. He knew that if she had, any chance of marrying her would truly be over. But luck, as usual, was with him. She seemed completely unaware. Puffing out his chest, he put on his most sympathetic expression and walked to her. "Belle, you know how loyal I am to your family," he said, laying on the sincerity, "but your father has been making some unbelievable claims."

"It's true," Jean said. "He's been raving about a beast in a castle."

Belle looked back and forth between the two men. *That* was why Maurice was being hauled off to an asylum? She nearly laughed out loud in relief. "But I have just come from the castle," she said quickly. "There *is* a beast!"

Reaching out, Gaston put a hand on her shoulder. Then he gave her a condescending smile. Ever the showman, he spoke as much to the crowd as to her. "We all admire your devotion to your father," he said, "but you'd say anything to free him. Your word is hardly proof."

Panic gripped Belle's heart. She needed something to show them that she wasn't making it up. But what? In the pocket of her dress, her hand closed around the mirror. "You want proof?" she asked. She pulled out the mirror and held it up to face the villagers. *"Show me the Beast!"*

Once again, the mirror face swirled magically. The reflection of the village faded away and was replaced by an image of the Beast. He sat slumped against the turret wall, the picture of dejection. "There is your proof!" Belle cried. Gaston's face grew pale with shock.

"Well, it *is* hard to argue with that," LeFou said, turning to look at his friend.

"This is sorcery!" Gaston shouted, snatching the mirror from Belle's hand. He held it up for all the villagers to see. "Look at this beast. Look at his fangs! His claws!"

The villagers craned their necks, hoping to get a better look, then recoiled when they caught sight of the Beast. Watching their reactions, Belle bit her lip nervously. She hadn't thought things through when she pulled out the mirror. She had been so desperate to save her father that it hadn't occurred to her what actually seeing the Beast would do to the villagers. She hadn't thought that they would see only the Beast's appearance, not the man inside she had grown to care for. "No!" she cried out, trying to fix the situation. "Don't be afraid. He is gentle and kind."

"She is clearly under a spell," Gaston called out, shooting Belle a look. "If I didn't know better, I'd say she even *cared* for this monster."

Belle felt his words like a slap across the face. After

all he had done, *he* dared call the *Beast* a monster? "The Beast would never hurt anyone," she said, turning and pleading with the villagers. They looked back at her, their expressions wary, and the unease in the pit of her stomach grew. She should have known better. The villagers loved their Gaston. He was their war hero, their unofficial leader. He was their one small claim to fame. And Belle? She was an odd girl who liked to read.

As Gaston continued to rile the villagers into a frenzy against the Beast, Belle backed away. She had lost all hope of turning the tide in her favor. Catching sight of her, Gaston shouted to three of his henchmen. "We can't have her running off to warn the Beast," he said. "Lock her up."

Before she could turn and run, one of the men grabbed Belle roughly by the arm. Belle kicked and shouted, but it was no use. As Gaston called for his horse, she was dragged and tossed into the wagon cell where her father was being held. Monsieur D'Arque moved to stand guard.

Throwing his leg over his big black stallion, Gaston

turned once more to the villagers. Shouts of approval rang out as he lifted his hand to the night sky. "That creature will curse us all if we don't stop him!" he hollered, riling the villagers up further. "Well, I say we *kill the Beast!*"

The village erupted in bloodthirsty cries as Belle watched in horror behind the iron bars. Gaston was in his element. *This* was what he lived for—chaos and destruction, mindless violence. The Beast wasn't just a scary monster to him; he was an enemy, and *this* was battle. As Gaston led the mob from the village, he stoked their fears until they were burning as bright and hot as the torches some of the men carried. He painted a picture of a slobbering creature that lived in the dark and shadows. A beast with razor-sharp fangs and massive paws. A monster that roared and foamed. A living nightmare that needed to be destroyed. By the time the mob had disappeared into the woods, they were carrying weapons of all shapes and sizes. Some held shovels; others seized pitchforks. A few found axes and hefted them over their shoulders. And *all* of them—armed or not—looked ready to follow Gaston in his wild plan to kill the Beast.

Unable to do anything else, Belle stood still, her hands clutching the iron bars. The Beast, Mrs. Potts, Lumiere . . . everyone she had grown to love . . . they were in serious danger. And it was all her fault.

CHAPTER XIV

INSIDE THE BEAST'S CASTLE, THE STAFF members felt as though they were already dead. Their one hope of salvation—Belle—had fled, and now the Beast was back to brooding, the rose was still wilting, and they had no chance of reversing the curse before it was too late.

As the night had grown darker, they had gathered in the foyer, taking solace in all they had left—each other. Mrs. Potts and Chip nuzzled together on the serving trolley while Plumette rested her head on Lumiere's shoulder. His flames had grown dim and his expression was as drawn and serious as that of Cogsworth, who stood off to the side.

"He has finally learned to love," Lumiere said sadly, gazing toward the window that looked out on the turret where the Beast sat.

"A lot of good that does us if she doesn't love him in return," Cogsworth pointed out. He crossed his arms and pouted.

Shaking her head, Mrs. Potts wheeled her cart closer to the grumpy clock. "No," she said. "This is the first time I've had any real hope she would."

Cogsworth opened his mouth to make a snippy retort but was stopped by Chip. The young teacup had turned toward the door and was listening intently to something. "Did you hear that, Mama? Is it her?" he asked, jumping down from the serving trolley and hopping over to the window.

The rest of the staff rushed to join Chip at the window. They strained against the windowpane, trying to hear whatever the young teacup had heard. In the distance, they saw light from torches flash through the trees.

Lumiere's flames erupted in excitement. "Could it be?" he asked, pushing through the other staff. It was hard to see outside through the frost that covered the window. He held up a flame, warming the window until the frost melted. Then he shouted, "*Sacre bleu! Invaders!*"

The others peered through the cleared window. Lumiere was right. It wasn't Belle coming through the woods, returning to the Beast. It was a mob! And from the looks of it, a very angry mob. The villagers pushed through the castle gate and made their way across the bridge up to the colonnade. Leading the charge was a tall, broad man on a black stallion. As the staff watched, he turned and addressed the mob.

"Take whatever treasures you want!" he cried. "But the Beast is *mine!*"

The staff collectively gasped in fear. What were they going to do?

Cogsworth knew exactly what *he* had to do. He had to warn the Beast. Leaving the others to form a small, sad barricade at the front door, Cogsworth headed to the turret. He hopped and wobbled his way up a dozen flights of stairs and down long halls before finally waddling out onto the balcony. Peering around, he tried to spot the Beast among the stone gargoyles that lined the balcony. He finally saw him perched near the far end. His head was down, his shoulders hunched.

Cogsworth cleared his throat. "Oh, pardon me, master," he said nervously.

"Leave me in peace," the Beast said, not bothering to look up.

"But the castle is under attack," Cogsworth said urgently.

The Beast still did not look up, his face cloaked in darkness. When he spoke next, his voice rippled with pain. "It doesn't matter now," he said sadly, finally raising his head. His piercing blue eyes were stormy and full of held-back tears. "Just let them come."

Cogsworth had had enough. Gone was the calm, patient, loyal majordomo. He had spent too many years stuck in his clock body to have his master give up now. He had watched the Beast throw away his only chance at happiness and he had silently let him. But not anymore. Now he was going to speak his mind. "Why fight?" he snapped. "Why indeed! Why do any bloody thing at all?" Finishing, Cogsworth caught his breath and waited for the Beast to say something, anything, in return. But all he did was once again lower his head.

With a sigh, Cogsworth turned and began the long walk back to the foyer. It looked like the staff members were on their own.

"I have to warn the Beast. . . ."

Belle looked around frantically. Her hands were clenched by her sides, and her eyes were wild as she desperately searched the small space for any means of escape. There wasn't one. The window was too tiny—and covered by bars—and the wagon had been locked from the outside.

"*Warn* him?" Maurice asked in confusion. He sat slumped in a corner. He looked worse than he had when he was a prisoner in the Beast's castle. His clothes were disheveled and his hair was sticking up in every direction. He had scrapes on his palms from falling on them, and exhaustion hung heavy on his shoulders. "How did you get away from him?" The last he had known, Belle was being held prisoner by the very beast she now wanted to protect.

Belle stopped pacing. She turned to her father and took his hands in hers. "He let me go, Papa," she said. "He sent me back to you."

"I don't understand."

Reaching into the small pouch she had taken from the castle, Belle pulled out the rose-shaped rattle. Maurice recognized it instantly. His hands began to shake as Belle told him how the Beast had taken her to Montmartre and had shown her their old home. Maurice took the rattle and moved it from one hand to the other as the realization of what it meant, what Belle now knew, hit hard.

"Belle," he began, "I had to leave your mother there. I had no choice, I had to save you—"

"I know, Papa. I understand." Belle's kind eyes met Maurice's. "Will you help me now?"

Maurice struggled to hold back tears that threatened to spill out of his eyes. His daughter had always been so caring and so forgiving. He just hadn't known until now how much *he* had needed her forgiveness.

"But . . . it's dangerous," Maurice said.

"Yes, it is," Belle answered bravely. She waited for him to argue. But her father simply smiled and nodded. Then he clapped his hands.

"Well, then," he said as he looked around the tiny wagon cell, "it looks like we need to find a way to get out of here so you can go save your beast."

Belle smiled. "Thank you, Papa." Then her smile faded. "But I've already checked. There's no way out."

Maurice shook his head. If he had learned anything over the years, it was that there was always a way out. He peered through the small window at the lock on the wagon door. Its makeup didn't look unlike some of his music boxes.

"I think I might be able to pick the lock, if only I had—"

Maurice suddenly saw the hairpin Belle was holding

up in front of him. There she was, anticipating his every need again. They shared a grin.

Then Maurice got to work picking the lock. When it finally clicked free, they slowly pushed the wagon door open.

"What are you waiting for?" Maurice whispered to his daughter. "Go!"

Giving him a grateful smile, Belle took off across the town square, not stopping to see if Monsiuer D'Arque had spotted her.

She made it to Philippe and hopped on the horse's back. Giving the big animal a strong kick, she pulled on the reins and steered them out of the village. Behind her she could hear D'Arque's angry shout and her father's happy cheer. Leaning forward, Belle urged Philippe on. They didn't have time to celebrate this minor victory. They needed to get back to the castle.

As they galloped through the thickening trees, Belle could only hope that they would get back in time. She didn't want to imagine what Gaston and his

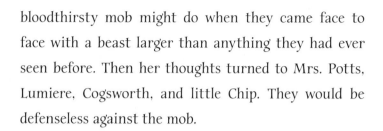

bloodthirsty mob might do when they came face to face with a beast larger than anything they had ever seen before. Then her thoughts turned to Mrs. Potts, Lumiere, Cogsworth, and little Chip. They would be defenseless against the mob.

CHAPTER XV

"ATTACK!"

Mrs. Potts's voice rang out through the foyer. On her command, the furniture around her came to life.

Despite Belle's fear, the staff members of the castle were far from defenseless. Or rather they were trying to be. As soon as they had seen the approaching mob, they had sprung into action. While Cogsworth had been trying, and failing, to get the master to stop wallowing and fight, Mrs. Potts, Lumiere, and Plumette had come up with a plan. It was simple—barricade the door—but it was a plan nonetheless.

They had tried to block the door, but when the villagers started breaking it down with a battering ram, they knew it was fruitless.

So they had decided to flee their post at the door and play to their strength, lying in wait, as still as real furniture, while the unsuspecting villagers poured in. Finally, Mrs. Potts yelled the signal, and the objects sprang into their surprise attack.

Chairs kicked. Plumette and the other dusters waved their feathers in villagers' faces until they started to sneeze. Candles shot their flames high into the air, blinding some and giving the backsides of several unsuspecting villagers quite the burn. As the furniture advanced, the mob shrieked in fear and the villagers tried to defend themselves. But the castle staff had the element of surprise.

Standing amid the chaos, Gaston tried to make sense of what was going on. He knew how to fight other men. He had done that plenty of times. He knew how to hunt animals. That, too, he had done. But a roomful of furniture that could walk and talk? That was something he had never encountered before.

"Gaston!"

Hearing LeFou's warning cry, Gaston turned to see a tall coatrack pulling back one of its "arms," preparing to hit him. Gaston didn't think. He just acted. Grabbing LeFou by his collar, he held the little man up in front of him. The coatrack's punch landed squarely in LeFou's midsection.

LeFou grunted. A moment later, things got worse as a large harpsichord stood on its back legs and fell forward. Once again, Gaston used LeFou as a human shield. There was a muffled shout as the harpsichord fell onto LeFou.

"Sorry, old friend," Gaston said, not bothering to help LeFou up, "but it's hero time."

"But . . . we're *Le Duo*. . . ." LeFou's voice grew weaker as the weight of the bookcase bore down on him. A moment later, he passed out.

Gaston took one last look at LeFou. Then he looked down at the mirror he still had clutched in his hand. He could see the Beast sitting on a turret somewhere high above the foyer. "Hero time," he repeated under his breath. He turned and raced through the furniture. He ducked out of the way as a small teacup blasted by him on the back of a serving trolley. He moved to the side as a credenza tried to trip him, and he avoided falling over a small bench that barked at him like a dog.

Moments later, he was bounding up the grand staircase as the noise of battle faded behind him. He kept climbing. His battle was somewhere ahead; he knew it.

Then, as if to prove him right, Cogsworth appeared at the top of the stairs. The small clock was descending from one of the turrets, his expression glum.

"My, my, what are *you* doing all the way up here, clock?" Gaston said. "Is there a beast up there?"

Cogsworth gulped. He had just inadvertently given away the Beast's position. Before Cogsworth could do anything to stop him, Gaston swung his leg back and kicked Cogsworth down the stairs. As Cogsworth thudded away, Gaston once again set his sights on the top of the turret stairs. Now that he knew the Beast was somewhere up there, it was only a matter of time before he had another trophy to mount on his wall.

Far below the turret, the household furniture continued to push back the villagers. Mrs. Potts poured boiling tea out of her spout while Chip, riding Froufrou, drew a dozen annoyed villagers toward the kitchen, where Cuisinier was waiting, pots of grease also ready to be poured. As soon as Chip was safely past, Cuisinier dumped the grease on the floor. A moment later, the villagers entered the room and instantly began to slip and slide. They fell into a pile on the floor.

Unbeknownst to anyone, a new figure was making her way through the chaos: Agathe the beggar woman. Though she wore her usual rags, she looked different than she normally did in the village. Her face was clean and the hair underneath her hood was formed into soft curls. She walked calmly past the droves of fighting villagers and objects, and ascended the staircase that led to the Beast's lair.

Meanwhile, Chip headed back to the foyer. He arrived just in time to see villagers flooding out the front door, screaming in fright. He was about to let out a triumphant shout when, out of the corner of his eye, he saw his mother swinging on the chandelier. Hot water continued to pour from her spout, spraying the fleeing villagers.

Suddenly, she slipped and fell through the air.

Mrs. Potts yelled.

Chip gasped.

And then, just when it looked like Mrs. Potts was going to shatter against the hard ground, a hand reached out and snatched her from midair.

It was LeFou! The little man had saved her! They stared at each other, both surprised by the sudden turn of events. "I used to be on Gaston's side," he said, shrugging apologetically. "But I'm just tired of being treated like an object, you know?"

"I do know, yes," Mrs. Potts said, smiling. "Now, shall we get back to it?"

As Mrs. Potts hobbled off to help the others, LeFou,

feeling lighter now that he had finally shaken off his abusive partner, peered around the foyer. Only a few villagers remained inside. Most had run away, and those who had stayed were being funneled out the front by a large talking candelabrum and his army of candles. LeFou watched as the front door slammed behind them. A moment later, the castle staff shouted triumphantly. The castle was saved!

And then Belle burst through the door.

The girl was breathing hard. Her brown hair fell about her face in waves, and her cheeks were red. But her eyes were cold and hard. Instantly, LeFou knew exactly who she was looking for. "He's upstairs," he called. Turning, Belle gave him the slightest of nods. Then she raced toward the grand staircase. "Oh, and when you see him, let him know that *Le Duo* is over," LeFou shouted at her back. "I'm Le Single now!"

When Belle had ridden through the castle's gate, she had been sure she was too late. She heard people shouting and saw villagers running. But she suddenly realized that they were running *out* of the castle. Hope had flared in her chest, and when she had finally made it through the front door, she had been thrilled to see that the castle staff, her friends, had won. They stood around the foyer, cheering and congratulating each other, as the villagers fled, proverbial tails tucked between their legs.

Then she had realized something was missing: the Beast was nowhere to be seen.

And the bad feeling in her stomach had rushed back.

Now, as she raced up the stairs, her heart pounded. All she could think about was getting to Gaston and stopping him before he could do something awful to the Beast. What-ifs flooded through her mind: *What if I had never left? What if I had just kept the mirror hidden? What if I'm too late? What if I never get to see the Beast again?* Her eyes filled with tears and she stumbled on the top step. She knew that if the Beast was gone, she would have no one to blame but herself.

She had seen where the Beast was when she flashed

the mirror in front of Gaston. She had recognized the large stone statues that lined the castle's highest turret. Since he hadn't been downstairs, and since LeFou had seemed confident Gaston was up there somewhere, Belle had a pretty strong feeling that she would find both Gaston and the Beast on that turret. Picking up the pace, she plunged down the long hallway and onto the walkway that led to the tower. Then she skidded to a stop.

She had been right. The Beast and Gaston were on the balcony. Their backs were to her, so they didn't see her arrive.

"Hello, Beast. I am Gaston," the hunter said smugly. "Belle sent me." He was holding a large gun, the barrel pointed straight at the Beast. Gaston's finger tightened on the trigger. "Were you in love with her?" Gaston asked, his lip rising in a sneer. The Beast said nothing. Instead, he turned his back to Gaston. "Did you honestly think she'd want *you*?" the hunter taunted.

Still the Beast said nothing.

And then Gaston fired.

Belle cried out as the Beast dropped over the edge of the turret. "What have you done?" She ran over and tried to push past Gaston. The large man reached out and grabbed her arm. She struggled to free herself, but his grip was too strong.

Staring down at her, he asked, his voice full of disbelief, "You prefer that misshapen thing to me . . . *when I offered you everything*?" His fingers dug into her skin, turning it red. Belle cringed. Gone was the patriotic war hero. The man standing in front of her had finally revealed himself as the true monster he was. "When we return to the village, you will marry me. And the Beast's head will hang on our wall!"

"Never!" Belle shouted. Perhaps Gaston's hand slackened for just one moment. Or perhaps shock made him temporarily weaker. Or perhaps it was something more magical than any of that. But whatever the reason, Belle was able to yank her arm free. Pivoting on her heel, she grabbed the barrel of Gaston's gun. Then she kicked him in the shin and yanked the weapon from him—hard.

Gaston wasn't about to let go of his gun, even if the person on the other end was his supposed future wife. He hung on to it as Belle swung it closer to the turret's edge. His feet slipped and slid as he struggled to find his footing on the cold surface. But the stones were slick from the snow that usually blanketed the castle, and some were even loose. Gaston cried out as his foot landed on one loose stone. Releasing the rifle, his hands flew into the air as he stumbled backward over the edge of the turret. Belle gasped, sure that she had just sent Gaston plummeting to his death.

But Gaston hadn't survived the war by sheer luck. The man had lightning-fast reflexes. Just in time, he managed to swing himself to safety through a window below. With a grunt, he landed on the spiral staircase that led to the turret. His rifle, in the meantime, continued to fall and finally came to rest on a stone footbridge a few stories down.

Instantly, Gaston was on his feet. He glanced out the window. He saw Belle running toward the spiral staircase. For the briefest of moments, he thought the worry and fear he saw in her eyes was for him. But following her gaze, he saw the real reason for her fear: the Beast. The hulking creature had survived his own fall and was climbing slowly down around a slightly lower turret than the one Gaston had just been on.

A fresh wave of anger washed over Gaston and he quickly began to run down the stairs. He heard Belle shout as she gave chase, but he ignored her, pulling his bow and arrow out of the quiver strapped to his back. Pausing at another window, he took aim and fired.

The arrow struck the Beast's thigh, burrowing deep.

The Beast roared in pain. Gaston started to smile, pleased his arrow had hit home. But his pleasure was short-lived, as the Beast reached down and pulled the arrow out. Then he disappeared around the turret and out of Gaston's view.

Suddenly, Gaston felt something—or rather, someone—tugging at his back. His attention momentarily distracted from the Beast, he whipped around to find Belle tearing at the quiver. Her thin fingers pulled at the leather holder as she desperately tried to break it free. When that didn't work, she resorted to grabbing the arrows. She began to snap them in half one by one.

Gaston raised his hand to strike Belle away but stopped himself. Out of the corner of his eye he saw that the Beast had reappeared and was leaping down from one parapet to another. His going was slow due to the wounds Gaston had inflicted. Each time he landed on one of the low stone walls, he groaned in pain. Still, he kept going.

Shoving Belle away, Gaston once again took up the chase. His footfalls echoed off the stone walls as he raced down the rest of the staircase. When he reached the bottom, he ran onto a bridge. Across the way he saw the Beast, paused, ready to swing himself onto another parapet. If he made it, he would be as far away from Gaston as the mazelike roof of the castle allowed.

The Beast reared back on his haunches . . . and leapt.

At the same time, Belle reached the Beast's lair. Racing out onto the balcony, she frantically searched the roofline for the Beast. She found him just as he jumped.

He flew through the air, his arms stretched out in front of him to grab the side of the stone wall. He barely made it. His grip started to slip.

And then Belle screamed, *"No!"*

"Belle?" the Beast said, turning as her cry echoed over the castle's roof. Their eyes met, and in that instant, the Beast was filled with a strength he didn't know he still had. He pulled himself to safety, then made his way toward Belle, leaping from parapet to parapet.

Unfortunately, he was also making his way back toward Gaston, who was lying in wait. The hunter had ducked between the gargoyles that lined a landing not too far from the Beast's rooms. He watched with disgust as Belle called out to the Beast, and he sneered when the Beast seemed to revive suddenly at the sight of Belle. Wrapping his hands around a thin stone spire, he pulled it until it broke off. Once again armed, Gaston waited for the Beast to come to him.

He didn't have to wait long. Focused on reaching Belle, the Beast didn't even bother to look around as he landed on the gargoyle-lined walkway. His long legs swept him across the stones, his eyes locked on the terrace where Belle stood.

Gaston waited until the Beast was just past him, and then he roared. Jumping out of the shadows, he brought the spire down on the Beast's back.

The Beast roared in pain but kept going.

Seeing the Beast's determination, Gaston felt another rush of anger. "Fight me, Beast!" he shouted, following him. He hit him again and again. With every blow, Gaston managed to slow the Beast, but no matter what he did, he could not stop him. It made him furious and he swung the spire harder. Finally, he managed to knock the Beast off balance. The Beast staggered down a small set of stairs and out onto another stone footbridge.

Gaston jumped down behind him and continued his assault.

Under the combined weight of Gaston and the Beast, the footbridge, which had not been used in years and had fallen into disrepair, began to shake and crumble. Neither man nor beast paid any attention. Gaston had seen something lying at the far corner of the footbridge—his rifle. And the Beast had seen how very close he was to Belle. If he could make it to the end of the footbridge, he would be in the cupola that stood parallel to his rooms. From there it was just one giant leap between him and Belle.

"Gaston! *No!*"

Belle's cry warned the Beast. He turned to see Gaston, spire lifted high, readying to strike the death blow. The Beast had had enough. He was not going to let Gaston stop him from reaching Belle, not when he was that close. In one swift move, he reached up and yanked the spire from Gaston's hands. Then he hurled it against the far wall. It shattered into a thousand pieces. Snarling, the Beast wrapped his paw around Gaston's throat and swung him over the edge of the crumbling footbridge.

"No," Gaston pleaded as his legs dangled in open air. "Please. Don't hurt me, Beast. I'll do anything."

For a long, tense moment, the Beast just stared at

Gaston. The Beast's features were twisted with rage and hate—for all the years he had been trapped in that form; for the man in front of him, who could see him only as a beast; for the time he had already lost with Belle and the fear that he might lose still more.

Then his rage and hate began to fade. Turning, he saw Belle looking at them, hope in her eyes. It seemed she believed he could do the right thing, that he could be the best version of himself. And suddenly, the rage and hate were gone. Slowly, he swung Gaston back over the bridge's wall and set him down. "Go," he said. "Get out."

As Gaston scrambled away, the Beast turned and locked eyes with Belle. In that moment, he didn't need to hear her to know she was proud of him. All he wanted, more than anything in the world, was to be next to Belle. Dropping down on all fours, he took a deep breath. He had just enough distance to get his speed up to make a leap from the bridge to the balcony—and Belle.

Seeing what he was about to do, Belle shouted, "No! It's too far!"

But she was too late. The Beast's hind claws dug into the stone and he pushed off. Gaining speed, his four paws pounded over the stone. And then . . . he leapt.

For a moment, he seemed to hover in the air, suspended over the abyss of emptiness between the castle's roofs. Then time sped up, and with a thud he landed safely on the balcony. Looking at Belle, he smiled. He had made it! Nothing could keep him from Belle now. . . .

Boom!

The Beast roared in agony as the sound of gunfire echoed over the castle.

On the crumbling footbridge, Gaston reloaded the rifle. He had grabbed it from where it had been hidden among the rubble. As Belle watched, hopeless, he aimed the gun once more, an evil grin spreading across his face.

Boom! He fired again. The bullet flew through the air and slammed into the Beast, who fell to the ground.

But Gaston's luck had just run out. His weight, the decay of the footbridge, and the heavy recoil of the rifle proved too much. Before he could even let out a triumphant shout, the stones beneath his feet gave way completely. In an instant, there was only empty air—and a long drop into nothingness—under him.

Lifting her head, Belle saw Gaston—and his horrible rifle—disappear in a cascade of stones.

CHAPTER XVI

BELLE WANTED TO BELIEVE EVERY-
thing would be okay, that the Beast would
be okay. But as she sat, his head cradled in
her lap, she knew time was running out. It had already
run out for Gaston, though that had caused her only
a momentary pang of regret. He had been a horrible
man. While she never would have wished his fate on
anyone, she would not bother to waste tears or time on
his memory.

The Beast, though, was another story. She didn't
want him to become a memory. She wanted him to stay
there, with her, alive and well. She wanted to tell him
how much he meant to her. She wanted to tell him how
sorry she was for inadvertently sending Gaston to the
castle in the first place. Yet looking down at him, she
knew that her chance to do that was quickly slipping

away. The Beast's breathing was labored and his eyes were shut tight, the pain clearly overwhelming his body. Softly, Belle reached down and ran her fingers along his cheek.

When the Beast felt her touch, his eyes opened. "You came back," he said, looking at her with pure love. He lifted his paw and brushed back a lock of Belle's hair.

"Of course I came back," she said, trying to fight the tears that threatened to spill onto her cheeks. "I'll never leave you again."

The Beast lifted his shoulders in the slightest shrug. Then he sighed. "I'm afraid it's my turn to leave," he said, his voice weak.

Belle shook her head. *No!* she wanted to shout. *Fight! Don't just give up! Not after all we've been through. It took me so long to find you.* Despite her best efforts, the tears began to fall. The Beast's head was growing heavier in her lap. As she stared down at him, she felt her heart already breaking. Against the odds, the Beast had shown her true beauty. He had shown her it was okay to be different. He had shown her it was okay

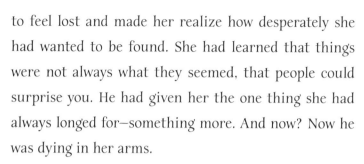

to feel lost and made her realize how desperately she had wanted to be found. She had learned that things were not always what they seemed, that people could surprise you. He had given her the one thing she had always longed for—something more. And now? Now he was dying in her arms.

Struggling for words, Belle choked back a sob. "We're together now," she said. "It's going to be fine. You'll see."

"At least I got to see you one last time," he said. As he spoke, his paw dropped from Belle's hair. His eyes closed. His breathing grew slower, and then it stopped altogether.

With another sob, Belle threw herself over the Beast's still body. He was gone. And she had never told him she loved him.

As the Beast took his last breath on the terrace above, his staff members, unaware of what had happened between their master and Gaston, were in the middle of a celebration. They had all gathered on one of the lower terraces to watch as the villagers ran off through the woods. Lumiere's flames were shining bright, buoyed by victory. Plumette had fluffed her feathers, and Cogsworth was ticking and tocking at a much faster rate than usual. Even the larger pieces of furniture, like Garderobe and her long-lost love, Cadenza, had made their way out to celebrate.

Lumiere turned to Plumette and took her in his arms. The feather duster giggled flirtatiously. "We did it, Plumette," he said, dipping her. "Victory is ours!" He leaned down to kiss her and gasped. She had grown still and silent in his arms. She was no longer alive. With the Beast gone, the curse had taken full effect.

One by one, the once animate objects grew inanimate. As Lumiere watched in horror, Garderobe froze in the middle of a theatrical flourish. Letting out a shout, Cadenza began to play his keys, frantic to keep them moving. But there was nothing he could do. They, too, slowed until, finally, they stopped and Cadenza became still. The curse swept through the castle like a wind, and no matter how they tried to escape it, the staff could not get away.

Froufrou barked one last time before turning back into a piano stool. Mrs. Potts frantically approached Lumiere and Cogsworth, searching for her son. But before she could find him, her face disappeared in the painted ornamentation of the teapot. Chip became still next, his features fading away until he no longer resembled a precocious little boy and was just a chipped teacup.

"Lumiere . . ."

Hearing Cogsworth's voice, Lumiere turned, dreading the inevitable. The little clock was struggling against the curse, trying his hardest to keep ticking. "No!" Lumiere cried. "Hang on, Cogsworth."

"I . . . can't . . ." Cogsworth said, his voice growing weak. He gave a long, slow tick and an even slower tock. "My friend, it was an honor to serve with you."

Lumiere lowered his flames as Cogsworth's voice faded completely. The only sound he made now was the ticktock of a small clock. He was no longer the major-domo. He was an object. And as Lumiere looked around, he saw that they were *all* objects now. No one but him was left. Lumiere knew that up in the master's lair, the last rose petal had fallen. A moment later he, too, stiffened and the light faded from his candles as his final transformation took place.

Soon the terrace was quiet except for the ticking of the clock that had once been Cogsworth. A soft snow began to fall, covering the objects and making them look like ghosts.

Up on the balcony, Belle barely noticed the snow falling on her head and shoulders. She didn't know that the curse had been enacted. All she could think about was the Beast, lying in her arms. His body still felt warm, and for a desperate moment, she wanted to believe that he was still there. She cradled his head in her hands. His fur felt soft in her palms and she wanted to force his eyes open so she could once again see them, the most beautiful blue she had ever known, staring back at her. "Please, don't leave me. Come back," she begged. Overcome with emotion, she slowly leaned over and placed a soft kiss on his forehead. And then, because she had never said it to him while he was alive, she whispered the words she had been carrying in her heart: "I love you."

Though Belle did not know it, Agathe had silently entered the room and was standing on the balcony next to what was left of the enchanted rose. The woman lowered the hood of her cloak and extended her hand toward the bell jar. In an instant, the jar disappeared, leaving behind the crimson petals and a trace of golden dust. Agathe swirled her hand and the petals rose. The golden dust seemed to multiply, moving rapidly toward the Beast, enveloping him entirely before lifting him off the ground.

Feeling the weight of the Beast's body lift from her lap, Belle looked up and gasped, seeing the golden haze swirling around his body. She noticed that the air felt warmer, thicker. Then, quite suddenly, there was a flash of light, and one of the Beast's paws turned into a hand. Belle stood, watching intently.

More bursts of light followed as the rest of the Beast's features turned into human ones. Finally, he landed softly on the ground, the transformation complete.

Silence fell over the balcony.

For a long moment, Belle stood where she was, her head spinning with what she had just witnessed. She stared in awe at the man standing in front of her. He was still wearing the clothes he had worn as the Beast. He had the same piercing blue eyes, though they were now wide and filled with concern as they looked upon her tear-stained face.

Belle's heart felt like it would burst with joy. She knew, deep in her soul, that this was the Beast she had grown to love, once again in his human form. And she knew, without hesitation, that she didn't want to waste another moment not being close to the one she loved. Blue eyes met brown, and then, as dawn broke over the horizon, they leaned forward and kissed.

It was a kiss Belle would never forget—one better than any in all the books she had read. It was a kiss full of apology, full of thankfulness, and full of deep, deep love. It was a kiss full of enchantment. And as their lips met, that magic exploded from them to the rest of the castle.

As the sun rose higher into the sky, the castle began to transform. The cold gray stone became awash with gold. The snow faded from the ground, giving way to bright green grass. Colorful flowers burst forth, and in the colonnade, the white roses turned red. Up on the parapets of the castle, the gargoyle statues, their faces so long stuck in frightening sneers, returned to their original forms of noble beasts and men. Even the sky seemed touched by the magical transformation. Clouds disappeared, revealing a sky almost as brilliant blue as the Prince's eyes.

Inside the castle, the transformation continued. As the light from the dawn filtered through the large windows, it illuminated the objects that had, only moments before, been rendered immobile. Froufrou turned from a piano bench back into a tiny bichon frise. Immediately, he leapt up and chased his tail before going to relieve himself on the immobile coatrack, who, as luck would have it, turned back into a man just as Froufrou finished his business. Shooing him away, the valet turned and almost tripped over the trolley cart holding Mrs. Potts and Chip.

He shouted as it started to roll away, barely missing Garderobe, who was waddling in and out of the sunlight. As she did, she turned from wardrobe to human to wardrobe again until, finally, she landed with a thud right next to Cadenza. Moments later, they both transformed once and for all back into the diva and the maestro.

And so it continued. Throughout the castle, excited cries could be heard coming from all over as the curse was lifted. Maids giggled as their feathers turned back into legs, and candles shouted happily as their wicks turned back into fingers. In the kitchen the stove became the chef again and immediately began giving orders to prepare a feast.

Cogsworth's ticks became a series of coughs as he, too, transformed back into his human shape. Brushing off his coat, he looked around for Lumiere and smiled when he saw that the candelabrum was once more head footman—but still up to his old tricks. He was chasing Plumette around the dining room table. Catching her, he dipped her back and kissed her passionately.

Cogsworth was saved from witnessing how long the kiss went on by the rattling sound of china. He looked up to see the trolley carrying Mrs. Potts and Chip barreling toward the top of the staircase. For a tense moment, it looked like they might tumble to their doom. But as Cogsworth watched, the trolley jerked to a stop, sending Mrs. Potts and Chip flying forward. Midair, as their fragile bodies hit the sun, they transformed, and they slid down the rest of the stairs on their very human posteriors.

"Oh, Chip!" Mrs. Potts cried happily. "Look at you— you're a little boy again!" Reaching out, she tried to give his cheek a squeeze. He ducked out of the way, like any little human boy would, and raced toward the front door. As he flung it open, the sun poured in—and so did some of the villagers.

For truth be told, they had been under the enchantment, too. Now, with every moment that passed, they were beginning to remember all they had forgotten: the castle with the cruel king and the haughty prince, the lavish parties that had once been thrown, their loved ones who had worked there.

Approaching the front door, Jean the potter took in the castle, which now glowed with happiness and warmth. And then his eyes fell on Chip in the doorway and, beyond, Mrs. Potts. He shouted happily, "Darling?"

Mrs. Potts smiled back. "Hello, Mr. Potts," she said, running toward him.

"Beatrice, Chip," he said as his wife and son fell into his arms. "I've found you."

The reunions continued. And standing in front of the castle, smiling to herself, was Agathe. She had only ever wanted to see the Prince become a kinder man. And as she watched his happy staff members run about the castle, calling out to one another, hugging one another, she knew that he had found a way to be kind. He had found his heart. It had taken some time and one particularly stubborn young woman to help him do it, but nevertheless, he had found his way.

Seeing that her work was done, Agathe smiled and turned, leaving as silently and mysteriously as she had arrived.

Meanwhile, Plumette let out a shout. Everyone turned toward the staircase. At the top, as if on cue, stood the Prince. Belle was beside him, and their eyes were locked in a look of pure love. The staff rushed to greet them.

"Hello, old friend." The Prince addressed Lumiere happily. Belle watched the Prince embrace each member of the staff—of his family, really—allowing him the moment that had been so long in the making. She sighed contentedly. All was as it should be.

EPILOGUE

BELLE HAD NOT THOUGHT IT POSSIBLE to be that happy. But she was that happy. Deliriously, wonderfully, blissfully happy.

Gliding across the ballroom in her prince's arms, she smiled as they passed faces now so familiar to her. She saw her father, free and healthy. She caught sight of Lumiere and Plumette dancing nearby. She saw Chip, wedged between his mother and father, pretending to be annoyed but clearly loving the attention. Cogsworth was there, as was the diva, Belle's former wardrobe. She waltzed happily with her maestro. *This,* Belle thought as she gazed around the room, *is my family.*

She lifted her head, and her eyes met the Prince's piercing blue ones. He smiled down at her and she felt the now familiar warmth of love shoot through her whole body, starting at her toes and traveling to the tips of her ears. Over the past few weeks, she had found herself loving the Prince more with each passing day as she watched him embrace the life that had been denied him for so long.

I'm living my own adventure, she thought as he swung her around. She had found a life outside the village, and there were still so many places to visit and experiences to be had. What's more, she had found a partner who wanted to travel, as well, a partner with whom she could share all these adventures. *And there is nothing more I could ever want. Except . . .*

Feeling Belle tense in his arms, the Prince looked at her, his eyes narrow with worry. "Belle . . ." he said. "What are you thinking?"

Belle took a moment to consider her answer and tried not to smile as the Prince's expression grew more worried. Then, reaching up, she ran a hand down his smooth cheek. "How would you feel about growing a beard?"

Letting out a roar of laughter, the Prince pulled Belle closer. His eyes locked with hers and he nodded, an unspoken promise to always try to be the best version of himself, the version she had believed was possible before he had. Then, leaning in, he kissed her. And as she closed her eyes and gave in to the magic of the kiss, the world faded away until it felt as if it were just the two of them, caught up in a tale as old as time. Belle thought about the future—about the reading classes she could teach in the castle library for all the village students, the traveling she and the Prince would make time for, the friendships with those in the castle that would undoubtedly be lifelong. A tale that had begun once upon a time and would end, Belle knew, happily ever after.